SURE STRIKE

Nigel Rock

Published by New Generation Publishing in 2018

ISBN:978-1-78719-688-9

www.newgeneration-publishing.com

New Generation Publishing

Acknowledgments

A number of people helped me with proof reading, translations and encouragement. Their help is gratefully acknowledged.

John Bradshaw
Helen Brown
Lewis Commander
Elizabeth Mitchelmore
Geraint & Thelma Morgan
Geoff Newnes
Keith Owens
Andrew Patrick
Carol Rock
Glesni Thomas

This book is dedicated to my late parents R G C Rock and D M Uff, to my mathematician daughter K S Rock and to the men and women of RAF Bomber Command.

Foreword

The story is fiction. Although fiction, a number of the incidents described are based on real events.

My late father was an orderly room sergeant in Bomber Command and described to me encountering a Welsh speaking recruit with very little English who seemed to be lost in the system. After a few weeks he disappeared back into the system again. He also told me that beer was considered to be a strategic supply (no doubt for morale purposes) and that he was involved in monitoring and auditing the proper control of supply. On one occasion he was called upon to explain to the Commanding Officer why the consumption and supply figures did not match – this was because of the ullage. The CO (himself a teetotaller for religious reasons) had limited experience of the beer trade!

Contemporary mathematicians founding Operational Research in WWII did calculate that improving flying speeds would reduce losses and suggested removal of the upper turret of some bombers.

There were schemes to assassinate Nazi leaders including Reinhard Heydrich (successfully) and Hitler (Operation Foxley).

There was initial reluctance in the RAF to rely generally on some of the electronic guidance systems. According to R V Jones, (who was the inspiration for Dr James in the story) there was a raid on a radar station at Florennes using the "Oboe" navigation aid and the fall of bombs was witnessed by the Belgian resistance to establish the accuracy of the system.

The RAF ran Mosquito flights to Sweden purporting to be civilian traffic, but usually carrying diplomatic bags and occasionally a (cramped) passenger, often returning with ball bearings.

My late mother was also in Bomber Command (where she met my father) and some of her fellow WAAFs found the men of the Polish squadrons to be enthusiastic and passionate!

The Enigma codes did rely on "pinches" of code books, hence the importance of the books obtained from Sweden in this story. Enigma messages were grouped in fours with X as blank. Many senior Germans considered Enigma to be unbreakable and preferred to think there were informers somewhere when sensitive material was apparently disclosed. There are rumours that the Welsh language was used to disguise messages in both WW1 and WW2 (and even in recent Balkan conflicts when the British Army was part of the NATO contingent).

In some circumstances, infiltrations of British agents repetitively went wrong by them falling into the hands of the Germans (notably in Holland) and the Germans utilised their capture to send false messages to the British.

The Leigh Light and the Molins cannon were enhancements added to anti-submarine aircraft. The Leigh Light was also used in the Dam Busters raids to set the flying height above the water surface.

Escaped POWs who made it across the border into Switzerland were allowed to leave Switzerland and eventually return home. Allied aircrew who made forced landings in Switzerland, as opposed to those who had escaped from POW captivity in occupied Europe, were interned for the duration.

Nigel Rock
Napton on the Hill
Warwickshire
nigel@rocksystems.co.uk

Chapter 1

In the steel grey dawn of a bleak October morning in 1942, Ron Cooper and Rhys Evans felt the chill of an easterly wind carrying a spatter of shower droplets. They stood on the roof of the stores building at the Lincolnshire Bomber Command airbase of RAF Whittingsmoor. Ron took his glasses off and wiped the lens with a damp handkerchief which he pulled from the pocket of his RAF-issue greatcoat. His hands and slightly numbed fingers wiped away at his wire framed lenses, but Ron's eyes were fixed on the horizon. His glasses were really for close work – he could see tolerably well at the distance, but not well enough to satisfy the MO for anything other than an admin role with the Royal Air Force.

As they watched, a line of heavy bombers circled round the airfield, erratically spaced but at an even height. The aircraft were silhouetted above the nearly straight horizon between the sky and the Lincolnshire fields, recently shorn of the harvest of vegetables. Rhys and Ron were counting. In a moment the aircraft would turn in line towards the runway and then keeping count would be impossible as the Lancasters masked one another when seen from the vantage point the two men occupied.

Rhys turned to Ron. Speaking in Welsh he said "*Rhifais 28–wyt ti'n cytuno?*"[1]

Ron replied in Welsh "*Ie 28 – ni'n dri yn bring o hyd*"[2]

---

1 *"I counted 28 – do you make it the same?"*
2 *"Yes 28 – we're still three short."*

Rhys held the lowest RAF rank of Aircraftsman and had been brought up in Mid-Wales at a remote spot where English was rarely heard – and never spoken by local people. Until conscripted into the RAF, being unable to speak and understand English had presented no handicap to his job as a shepherd on the Welsh hills.

"Disgwyl dyna'r tri diwethaf!"[3] Rhys pointed to the back of the column of aeroplanes, where one, trailing smoke, was following a different and uneven climbing course towards the sheds of the aerodrome which was obviously not any sort of normal approach to the runway. It was already much higher than the others and as it became less of a dot and more of that distinctive shape of the big bomber viewed from head on and below, it was clear that a struggle for control must be challenging the pilot.

*

Every man inside the damaged Lancaster knew what it was like to be in a cold sweat. The numbing damp cold at operational altitude, even in the big fleece-lined flying suits, got to everyone, but this homeward leg had been an extended period of stomach-churning anxiety. Their skipper, of Squadron Leader rank, was Simon Askew, a man who had flown 14 operational missions and brought his aircraft back safely every time. Until now. Ironically this should have been one of the less hazardous flights. They had been to southern Denmark and managed to avoid both flak and fighters by flying a roughly triangular course, planning a return on a more northerly route than the outbound leg. That return leg had been fraught for skipper and crew.

Their problems began just after dropping their bombs. Askew had guessed what had happened within about half a minute of the jarring lurching shock that pulled the stick from his grasp and forced the aircraft into a twisting earthward trajectory. A surge

3 *"Look there are the last three!"*

of adrenaline and an assault on the senses made the next few seconds proceed as if in a slow-motion film, as his mind raced. There was noise from the increased rush of air outside and the crazy spinning of the altimeter needle, with the other instruments assuming uncomfortably unfamiliar appearances to what was in reality a quick scan of the panel. Even while he struggled with the controls in the pitch darkness, he knew they had been struck by bombs falling from another bomber above them. This sort of incident was all too common, with many bombers in several streams – invisible, yet close, in the darkness. Pilots often felt the swirling slipstream of the others they could not see, until lit up by the fires of the target below. Even so, being bombed by your mates had an impact somehow more unexpected than an enemy attack.

Askew fought the strange responses from the machine to the controls, which now had quite different characteristics than those of moments before. By shear brute force he managed to recover from the half spin, put the thing into an approximation of level flight and found with some surprise that they were heading due west at 1000 feet. They may have found themselves pointing in the right direction, but there were hundreds of miles of North Sea between them and home. The Lancaster was misbehaving, weaving and pitching. Askew got the crew got ready to bale out. Unappealing as a long 'holiday' as a POW might seem, they would soon be out over the sea with little prospect of rescue from either side, even if they made it into a life raft. Suddenly with a jolt, the aircraft ceased pitching. Although the rudder was hard over and the gauges told Askew that one engine was out, surprisingly, they were flying a relatively steady course and height. Askew held a rapid discussion with the co-pilot and flight engineer. They concluded that some damaged bits of their aeroplane must have been flapping about before finally coming adrift. He briefed the crew over the intercom, who responded with a damage report. All the guns and turrets were working. Both from the instruments and from the behaviour of the aircraft Askew guessed the damage was confined to one wing, although in the dark, he could not be certain. The crew trusted his judgement, he knew. He decided to risk the 300 miles over open water.

Askew and his co-pilot had their hands full, but it was manageable. He dare not risk gaining height and they flew on, 1000 feet above the waves that they could not see, until little by little the gloomy night gave way to the coming dawn. The crew endured their cold sweat with little to do. The gunners kept look out and the navigator studied his watch, as it ticked away the seconds and the miles. Everyone kept their silence and their thoughts.

After an age, the Norfolk coast came in sight in the feeble light. The navigator noted their passage into air space over the fields of East Anglia somewhat earlier than he had calculated. He watched with a grateful grunt to himself, as the cliffs of Cromer passed under the port wing – the tail wind had freshened. There was a noisy exhalation of relief and release of tension from the crew. Askew dampened their optimism. It was known for enemy aircraft to loiter around their home bases – when nearing home they must not lower their guard, he reminded them.

Askew's struggle with the controls across the sea had been manageable with the help of the co-pilot. Could he land it? Should they bale out now? The upper turret gunner could now see the damage. He reported 'A bloody great hole in the wing'.

They neared Whittingsmoor. Around them, in the distance, other Lancasters from the squadron could be seen. He would let them in first. As they turned for an approach into the wind, something went wrong. The aircraft began to shake and shudder, weave and pitch. A controlled landing that had seemed fully possible for the last hour was now out of the question. Askew's fight with the controls resumed. His brain seemed to divide itself – part of him reasoned calmly that something had probably come loose in the wing, while he suppressed the natural fear that wanted to take over his body. Now there was a fire warning light in the remaining good engine on the damaged wing.

He managed to make the aircraft climb and ordered the crew to get ready to bale out as soon as they had sufficient altitude.

*

As Rhys and Ron watched, two figures tumbled from the bomber, quickly followed by another three. Suddenly the crippled aircraft executed a sharp upward pitch. Ron, his eyes riveted to the aeroplane, began counting again – this time willing the rest of the crew to make it out as parachutes bloomed in the sky above those that had already managed their exit. The big aeroplane stalled, turned somersault, but in its wake two more figures could be seen, free from the machine as it headed in an arc towards the open fields to the north west of the airfield. The Lancaster seemed to be making a slow cartwheeling motion as it headed towards the ground trailing smoke in a spiralling pattern. There was a flash followed by a tremor that shook the buildings as the doomed aircraft impacted the fields about a mile away. A few seconds later the sound of a rumbling explosion reached the ears of men and women stationed at RAF Whittingsmoor.

Ron and Rhys glanced at one another soundlessly for a moment. Ron knew that it was unusual to get all the aircraft back from a raid and even more unusual if there were few casualties among the returning bombers that did make it back. It was an open secret among the ground and air-crew that losses were high, even though the top brass never let anyone know the exact number. The numerical level of the crews that did not come back was something not really discussed in the mess or billets. There was emotional attachment – or emotional loss – and always the hope that crews had diverted to another base. That was talked about. For most, not knowing the actual numbers made it easier not to think about the risk too much. Ron however, did think about the numbers a lot.

Ron Cooper was an orderly room Sergeant, not directly involved in ops, but he took an interest in the numbers. He had to get the stores to run the base, its bombers, all sorts of bits and pieces and even the beer. In many ways the numbers were his business even if the ops and intelligence were not supposed to be his bailiwick.

This time it looked as if they had all got back – except that was, for the crashed Lancaster that had nearly made it. Ron pondered on this mission's good luck.

Rhys interrupted his thoughts of the wider implications on the return of the raiders, to focus on the immediacy of the crash. *"Dyna stwr ofnadwy!"* Ron couldn't make out the Welsh this time. "What?" Ron asked. Rhys repeated it, then again hesitatingly translating it into English: "That's a big bang!"

"Yes, Rhys but they're all back this time" Ron said reverting to English. "You should be speaking English by the way – you're supposed to be learning." He looked away from the column of smoke and flames, back to the runway with the landing bombers and he scanned the sight of trucks and Jeeps rushing about to greet the crews. Some would be going off the aerodrome to find the crew that had parachuted into the Lincolnshire countryside. Much of the wreckage would be scattered across the county boundary into Leicestershire and both the civil defence force and the RAF teams would be involved in recovery operations. Ron would have to work on the reports.

"Rhys, you cut along to the dining room and have your breakfast."

It was Rhys' turn to say "What?" He stood with his open coat flapping in the stiff breeze, in contrast to Ron who was buttoned up to resist the elements. Rhys repeated Ron's order in a quizzical tone. "Cut along?"

Ron replied "Cut along – it means walk – walk over to the dining room. Get your breakfast."

"Yes Sarge – will do. How can you learn Welsh quicker than I learn English?"

Ron, a university graduate, at 23 was five years older than Rhys. Ron had always been a quick learner. Ron's school teachers would have found they had a star pupil when it came to all types of languages – in fact his ability to pick up foreign tongues was completely exceptional. This talent had been somewhat suppressed as a school pupil as the headmaster took little interest in foreigners and foreign languages. What was of more interest to them was Ron's ability at maths which was noted as outstripping his latent ability with languages. Ron knew that Rhys was catching up quickly on his total lack of use of English until a few months ago. Not answering his question, Ron said "I could ask why you're not feeling the biting easterly wind. Go on – I'll come along when I've seen the last one touch down."

The dining room at Whittingsmoor was an open plan affair, divided into three sections; Sergeants, Returning Air Crews and other ranks. The Officers mess bar was a cramped extension attached to the building. As Ron entered the dining room, the catering team was serving breakfast to a general hubbub of backchat and laughter born of relief for those in any way associated with the night's op.

Ron seemed to pick up responsibility for all sorts of activity – anything not related to ops – including food supplies and the thorny task of keeping the catering up to scratch. In this endeavour he had struck lucky. The RAF's usual process of assigning cooks to gunnery and road sweepers to cooking had broken down. Jim, the catering supervisor who reported to Ron, actually had catered in large hotels before hostilities commenced.

As Ron came over to the counter, Jim was there with the ladies dishing up breakfast. Jim said "Just like you wanted Sarge, the boys coming back get theirs all together as soon as they walk in." He gestured expansively towards the rumbustuous air crew.

Ron looked round the room. "Yes it seems to be working okay. Have you seen Bob – the Met office Sergeant?"

Jim replied, "Yes, over there in Sergeant's mess."

Ron said "Okay let's have some breakfast, but leave the eggs off – I can't stand them!" Collecting his breakfast and steadfastly avoiding going anywhere near any eggs, he moved over to the tables in the Sergeants' section.

Bob Neal was the sergeant who ran the weather watch. His opinion attracted huge interest from the crew before an op, less so when it was over. Ron asked "Morning Bob – may I join you?"

Bob said "Sure, help yourself." I hear you've been doing something to the catering supplies. Good job. It seems to have got a bit better lately, but can't you do anything about the tea? It's as weak as dishwater!"

Ron smiled at the nearest thing to a compliment in the vexed area of food and catering. "I'll see what I can do." He paused. "Bit of a change in the weather this morning, Bob."

Bob sipped his mug of tea. "Yes – well – didn't get the forecast quite right, but not too far off. There's a low pressure area that moved quite quickly and changed the wind direction overnight."

"That would have been while the boys were out on the raid."

"Yes – wind was from the southwest but it swung round quite quickly, so we now have a steady breeze of 15 to 25 knots from the east this morning. You know that the wind circles round the low pressure areas I suppose?" Bob gestured with the stem of his pipe towards the east in case anyone was not sure where the source of this morning's wind as well as the Ruhr and all things Teutonic might lie.

Wind direction affected many things including some that the ground base personnel could not see, but take off and landing always involved flying into wind. Ron went on "Yes – I see they took off towards the village, but then landed coming back the same way – means they have to fly in a circuit around the airfield both times, with a turn over the village. Bet the locals don't like it." Ron ate some of his cooling breakfast whilst Bob fiddled with his pipe. Ron resumed "Just out of interest, can you remember the wind being like this before? I mean recently?"

Bob queried "What do you mean – cold wind from the East? It's not that uncommon."

"No, not quite. I mean the wind changing during a raid so they've got a tail wind out and a tailwind back."

Bob rummaged around in his pockets, evidently looking for a match. "Ah – gotcha. I'll have a look at the records when I get back to my desk. I'll give you a call. Mind you – I think you might be busy today – new boss is arriving tomorrow morning isn't he?"

Ron said "Yes, Group Captain Ryland, due about ten or eleven hundred I think."

"Ten or eleven?" Bob Neal, like most people that had dealings with Ron, found him thorough and something of a pedant for accuracy. He made a friendly jibe. "Bit imprecise for you. You usually know everything and fix everything. Do you know anything about Ryland?"

Ron had not had either the time or inclination to find out with the precision Bob was ribbing him about. "I will take him as he comes." He passed a bit of paper to Bob. "A list of dates for that wind question. Might make it easier for you."

Bob continued the jibe about Ron's famed attention to detail "You keeping weather records as well? You don't have to know every single thing about the place!"

Ron grinned and Bob rose to leave, lighting his pipe as he did so. "Get the new boss trained Ron!"

Ron called after him "Just try those dates – we'll talk later. And thanks!"

*

The RAF Regiment guards at the gate of RAF Whittingsmoor were checking a stack of leave passes when they saw a car approaching the gate, stopping at the barrier. Inside the car they could see an attractive blonde in the back seat. "Hello, what have we got here?" said one of the guards as the other got up, and with rather more enthusiasm than usual, jogged down the three steps of the guardhouse and approached the car. Just before making a remark he might have regretted later, he glimpsed the uniform of a senior officer seated on the other side of the car and realised that this must be the new CO. The driver wound down his window and produced his ID. As the guard took it, an elegant female hand appeared over the driver's shoulder holding two more Identity Documents for Group Captain John Ryland and WAAF Section Officer Joan Newcombe, evidently the owner of the hand. Quickly reverting to a more formal demeanour, the guard checked and returned the passes and snapped off a salute "Thank you Sir, Ma'am. You're expected." This was only partially true in the mind of the guard, as the day's orders listed the Group Captain and another unnamed Officer – but a dishy 25 year old blonde WAAF Officer was not what he had expected. He said to the driver "Turn right in 300 yards and you will see the main building ahead. He turned and raised the barrier, saluting the departing car, before returning up the steps. "New CO." he said flatly to the other guard who immediately picked up the telephone to warn the welcome party.

Whittingsmoor had been built in the 30s and the front facade of the main building made from a light-coloured Derbyshire stone, reflected the architectural styles of the time. As the car drew up the front steps of the main entrance Squadron Leader Simon Askew was waiting to greet them. If Askew had any after affects from his bale out less that 36 hours before, they didn't show.

While the driver opened the door for Joan Newcombe, Group Captain John Ryland hardly waited for the car stop before getting out. Ryland was not a man who liked to hang about and at 47 was quite a bit older than the air force he served. He was certainly a lot older than most of the officers and men under his command and although he had the classic formalised look of an older RAF officer, he exuded a sprightly active enthusiasm. Certainly to the men flying missions in bomber command, where 23 was old, he was positively ancient but somehow this was not noticed as he strode about the place giving out a "can do" air to all around him. "Morning Squadron Leader – it's Simon Askew isn't it?" he said as he bounded up the steps.

Askew replied “Yes sir.”

Ryland gestured towards Joan Newcombe with an outstretched arm. “Squadron Leader Askew meet Section Officer Joan Newcombe. She will be based here for a while checking up on the WAAFs on the stations in the Group.”

Simon Askew led them into the building with a “Come on through, Sir, Miss” and into the hall. Opposite the main door was a sign with the crest of Bomber Command which featured lightning bolts and wings over its motto ‘Strike Hard – Strike Sure’. They mounted a rather impressive stairway and on the first floor, turned into a short corridor. Askew opened the door to a large bright office overlooking the main runway in the distance. John Ryland tapped the engraved brass plate on the door which already announced ‘Group Captain John Ryland Commanding Officer’. He said “That was quick – is everything so efficient here?”

Askew replied “We try to be sir. Briefing documents are on your desk.”

Ryland walked round the desk sat down on the revolving chair, and gave it a spin. He turned back to face the desk and placed both palms face down on the table each side a writing pad “Right let’s get started. First thing we need is tea.”

Askew picked up the telephone on the corner of the group Captain’s desk “Polly come in and meet everyone – we’re going to need some tea.”

There followed a brief tour around the main block to familiarise Ryland and Joan with the layout. It became clear that Joan’s role would be a review of the female contingent at the RAF station. Most of them worked in administration although a few were involved in close work and maintenance and some dealing with matters such as stores and other engineering support. After the short tour, Joan disappeared somewhere with one of the senior WAAFs, while Ryland and Askew returned the CO's office.

Ryland produced papers from a document case he had been carrying. "Right. I read all the briefing stuff about the operations side over the last couple of days. I think you've been running the show Simon." he gestured towards a chair.

Askew drew up the chair "As far as the ops are concerned Sir, since Flight Lieutenant Jamieson went missing."

Ryland frowned "Yes – three months in charge I think and I see losses have been up and down a bit."

Shifting slightly uncomfortably in the chair Askew said "Well sir – depending on the targets, weather, and a slice of luck I should say."

Ryland leaned back " Well – relax I'm not going to change things around – at least not for a bit – seems you've been doing a good job and I'd like to get other commands up to your standard before we do anything – until I know what's what – I need to get my knees under the table. First thing is to understand how the base works. "

Askew said "Sir, you need to speak to Sergeant Cooper. He runs everything on the base from an administration point of view."

Ryland asked "Who is the officer in charge?"

Askew shifted in his chair "Oh well sir, it's a long story but there isn't one. Sergeant Cooper took over from a Flight Lieutenant Jamieson."

At the second mention of the name Jamieson, a flicker of attention, or concern, or both briefly showed on Ryland's face, although Simon Askew just continued. "Jamieson was transferred to another base after some difficulty with the accounts. He got killed on active service. He was popular with the team here it was all a great shame. In fact that's how Cooper got here."

Ryland leaned forward "Tell me about Cooper."

Askew said "Well sir, Cooper was conscripted soon after finishing a mathematics degree. Someone in the recruiting office decided that he hadn't been to the right university or something, and he didn't get a commission. Just at that point they wanted somebody to investigate our little accounting problem and they picked on Cooper because they thought he would be good with numbers. In fact it seems he's pretty good with everything – an enquiring mind and efficient organiser, and he has all sorts of ideas for improvements. He seemed to get on top of the system after quite a short time and can more or less fix anything in supplies and that sort of thing."

Ryland asked "What was the accounting problem?"

Askew replied "Cooper can give you the details – the rest of us never quite knew.

Ryland picked up the telephone. "Well, no time like the present." Askew could hear the phone ringing distantly in the next office where Polly – the CO's secretary – had her desk. As she answered Ryland spoke "Polly, can you get Sergeant Cooper up here straight away please."

Askew went on, "The local police in the area had had their eyes on a couple of spivs who live the high life – somewhat beyond their means. They are known as the Smith Brothers. The bobbies found a beer barrel in a ditch and traced it to the base here. It started a hue and cry and somehow the accounts didn't add up.

Anyway Jamieson was transferred away and was killed in a raid after saving his crew."

Ryland looked out of the window to where an aircraft was taxiing in the distance.

Askew continued with the few more details as he had heard of them. "Jamieson was involved in a pretty heroic action apparently. Quite in character – he never really wanted to run the orderly room but he caught some shrapnel in the leg and it took a long time to heal. In a way he was partly glad to get back into action as the circumstances weren't good for him here."

A few minutes later, there was a knock on the door and Polly appeared. From his angle Askew could see through the open door to where, some way behind Polly, Ron Cooper was straightening his forage cap. "Sergeant Cooper to see you Sir."

Ron Cooper marched in as formally as he could manage. Being regimented wasn't his strong point. He clicked his heels together and saluted. Ryland spoke first. "Hello Cooper. I'll be here as base commander a while and Squadron Leader Askew tells me you're the key man in running things round here."

Ron said stiffly "Thank you sir. I do my best."

Ryland "At ease. How does it all work then? I want to know about how the station runs. Give me a bit of a summary."

Ron wondered how he could describe everything he did in 30 seconds. "Sir, most of the admin is run from the orderly room. I have two WAAFS and two Airmen to assist me with various aspects of supply, personnel, running the facility and so on. We don't get involved in the Ops side, but help them to get replacement parts, fuel, consumables. That sort of thing. We order, log and account for most things on the station from big stuff like new aircraft, down to paperclips."

Askew interjected in a way he hoped was helpful. Sergeants didn't expect to be interviewed by a Group Captain that often. "Yes, that's right. Getting any sort of material to keep the Ops going is a challenge, and Cooper's a bit of a whizz at getting all the stuff we need. I don't know how we managed without him."

Ron responded. "Thank you, sir. Kind of you to say so. We also look after things like the NAAFI, food and we also have a relationship with the local pubs. The Ministry of Supply wisely decided that beer was a critical material and we organise supply from the brewery to the pubs."

Ryland said "Tell me about this investigation."

"Investigation Sir?

Askew thought that Ryland was surprisingly interested in the investigation with everything else that need to be sorted out.

Ryland said "Yes, I understand that there was an investigation into – what shall we say – irregularities…."

Ron looked sideways at Askew "If you say so, sir. The previous Group Captain wanted it hushed up. So I'm not sure what I should say." Ryland followed his eyes towards Askew.

Askew, sensing the mood said "I think I'm getting the message here –would you excuse me sir? Things to do."

Ryland replied "Yes – I shall see you later. Thank you, Askew." As Askew left the room, quietly closing the door behind him, Ryland continued "Sit down. So what's the story Cooper?"

Ron summarised "When I got here, a Military Police investigation had been going on. The filing and records were in a dreadful mess. I don't suppose they were perfect before, but by the time the MPs had finished, and they had turned over every drawer and file – it was difficult to find anything. A bit over the top for a small suspected offence you might think. Basically, the military police thought there was something going on with the supply of beer. The amount bought didn't match the amount sold, so they assumed someone was pinching it. Local spivs – the Smith brothers – were suspected but with an insider on the base. What they didn't find out about was the ullage allowance."

Ryland asked "What's that?"

Ron went on "Beer ferments in the barrel and some of it is unusable. It's quite normal in the brewing industry. Our local brew – highly thought of – tends to lead to a more than average loss through settlement, cleaning out the pipes and that sort of thing. It seems the MPs got it in their head that there was fiddling going on and the buck stopped with Flight Lieutenant Jamieson. Sir, my report cleared him of all suspicion."

Ron paused, seeing some sort of ambivalent reaction from the CO to his summary of recent history. There was more to tell about the investigation, but Ryland spoke a bit more quietly than before "Can I have a copy of that report?"

Ron replied "Well sir, I had orders to return all copies to the Group Captain – who sent them off to Personnel. So that's what I did."

Ryland asked "So you haven't got a copy at all?

Ron realised this was a potential trap "Obviously, I obeyed the orders sir, but…."

Ryland picked up on Ron's hesitation "But if I wanted to know what was in it……."
Ron was treading carefully. He had only just met Ryland and he was a very senior officer. On the other hand Ron had done a bit of homework on the new CO and the grape vine reported that he was a decent sort. Ron said "I don't have the actual report…" He paused and watched for the Group Captain's reaction and saw him nodding slowly in anticipation. "Well I might still have a rough draft Sir. I'll see if I can find something."

Ryland smiled "Good man! I see we'll get on. So what about the beer barrel in the ditch?"

Ron said "Ah, so you know about that Sir? Well it was a red herring in one way, but then not in another. The lorry drivers had all been given a talk about conserving petrol, and one of them decided to try and reduce the number of trips by stacking extra empties on top. It literally just fell off the lorry – a pure accident. But going through the books of this and the other stations in the Group showed that the police suspicion was well founded. I traced back through all the accounts and records and found that the fiddle was meat not beer. And meat is controlled by the civvies at the Ministry of Supply locally – not our direct responsibility – so our Flight Lieutenant could not be expected to find any errors."

Ryland interjected "But you did."

"I was looking – searching – for something." Ron continued "We have the supplies on a different footing now. And the Smith brothers have been nicked for it."

"It seems to me that you cleared Jamieson's name," observed Ryland.

Ron sensed the conversation was about to end. "I was pleased to do so Sir. We had never met – he was just name a to me, but by his reputation he was well liked and committed to the fight. It seems a pity he was killed before all this got sorted out."

He hadn't said, but Ron had been irked that man's name had not really been fully cleared, since the report had been kept confidential and the full outcome was not general knowledge. He could only speculate that the whole episode was an embarrassment that someone wanted swept under the carpet.

Ryland wound up the discussion with a remark about the 'rough draft' of the report and a wink. Ron thought he had probably taken the right tack and got off to a good start with the CO. Thoughts were forming in his mind and a friend in high places would be just the ticket.

Chapter 2

The orderly room at Whittingsmoor was probably better than most in Bomber Command, having been built, like the rest of the RAF station, before the restraints on time and material implied by wartime construction. It was divided up by part-height and some full-height screen walls that were timber framed and ribbon glazed. Distorted multiple images of whoever was on the other side could be made out. This morning when Ron came in, the images he could see were of many blonde haired women in uniform moving in a choreographed dance like a parody of Busby Berkley set. The source didn't look like Sally or Sybil from his team, nor any of the WAAFs normally to be seen around. He put his head round the corner.

The blonde was in conversation with the girls in the outer office. Ron was expecting to see an officer called Joan Newcombe, but not the attractive vision he saw before him. The vision said "Good morning, you must be Sgt Cooper." The WAAF rank of Section Officer had to be worked up to through the other ranks, so Ron had been expecting an older, battleaxe type.

Ron said "Yes ma'am. Good morning. Would you like to come into the office?" opening his door and showing her in.

Joan took a seat and crossed her legs. "I think you know I have been given the job of checking up on the welfare of all the WAAFs in the group. Your gals here seem to think a lot of you. I think you keep personnel records of all the WAAFs on the airfield here – yes?"

Ron tried not to think about, nor to look at, the legs. "Yes ma'am we do, plus some from the other airfields in the group." He pointed to some filing cabinets.

Joan said "I suppose I shall have to find my way around those files then. I imagine I shall be here a while. I hope we are going to get on."

He slightly raised one eyebrow. "I shall look forward to that."

His unsaid comment earned a rebuke that was clearly not meant. "Don't be clever with me Cooper – no matter how clever everybody else thinks you are."

She got up, straightened her skirt and left with an "I'll see you later."

Ron was just recovering from this brief but memorable exchange when Bob Neal appeared at Ron's office door. He had clearly passed Joan on his way in.

"Wow Ron, who is the dishy blonde?"

Ron dropped into his chair "She is a WAAF officer come to check up on the welfare of the gals. We didn't discuss the weather."

Bob grinned "Well, send her round to see me and we'll see what the forecast holds." Bob had a manila file in his hand which he dropped on the desk. "Anyway, speaking of forecasts – how did you come up with the dates you gave me, because you guessed right – every time a tailwind out and tail wind back, more or less. Either that or a possible routing to avoid headwinds"

Ron looked pensive "Just keep it to yourself at the moment, but those were the sorties when we had very few losses. When you look at the figures those sorties stand out. I thought if we could pinpoint some sort of reason we might be able to reduce our casualty rate. I reckon the reason is the speed over ground."

Bob flicked through the file. "This would only make a few knots difference. You wouldn't have thought getting in and getting out a little bit quicker would account for anything."

Ron said "No – neither would I." He paused. "Do you know anybody in air defence?"

"Strange as it may seem I don't know anybody in German air defence." Bob spread his arm outwards.

Ron responded "Clot! I mean on our side – they're in the same game of intercepting incoming aircraft – the opposite team of course. Hang on, Sally used to be in the fighter command plotting room – she might know something."

*

The few grassed areas around the building at Whittesmore were criss-crossed with tarmac paths. As Ron walked towards the hangers the next day he encountered Joan who was on a converging path going in the same direction.

She hailed him "Hello Sergeant Cooper. Can you show me the way to the repair hanger?"

Ron slowed his stride as the paths met "Yes ma'am. The maintenance hangar – it's this way." They walked together and began to converse about the base and how it operated in terms of personnel. "There's a few girls in there – some civvies and three WAAFs. The WAAFs raise orders for materials, repairs and so on, then we set about getting the stuff they need."

It was a hundred yards or so to the hanger. Joan asked "What's the story with the Welshman?"

Ron said "Ah! Aircraftsman Second Class Rhys Evans. I suppose the girls in the orderly room told you something."

Joan said "I'd like to hear it from you."

Ron explained "Evans appeared a few months ago. His records show he had been run around a bit. He comes from the hills of mid Wales – somewhere called Croesor Crossing – an isolated hamlet, it seems – with just a railway halt and a few houses. He was a farmer cum shepherd. It's a totally Welsh speaking area. He had to take his call-up papers to the vicar for them to be read to him. Not because he can't read – but because he had no English at all. The vicar said 'You will have to go Rhys'. When all you have known is working as a hill farmer there was no need to learn English – until he joined the Air Force.

Joan drew a comparison "We've got used to whole squadrons of Poles and Czechs, but I guess we organise translators there."

Ron nodded as they walked "Yes. We've got a Polish squadron in our group – still I suppose you knew that."

Joan did know that "Of course. One of my jobs is keeping my gals out of the clutches of the more amorous members of the squadrons and the Polish boys can be more passionate than most."

Ron also was aware of the Poles socialising "Quite! The Poles are passionate about their country and a great asset, but I hear they make their mark with the ladies as well. Anyway, Evans had had a bewildering time. Seems he was just moved on from one station to another. They didn't know what to do with him. I thought I might teach him English and fixed him up with a bit of fetching, carrying, transport, general support, that sort of thing.

They passed an Aircraftsman going the other way who saluted Joan.

Joan was curious "So you speak Welsh?"

Ron said "Not before I met Evans. I taught myself Welsh. I knew a bit of French but my main foreign language is German.

Joan thought there was more to Cooper than met the eye. "German! Does the Air Force make use of it?"

Ron replied "No – well not as yet. I did a degree in mathematics at Leicester University. It's a fairly new university. Did you know there are lots of great German mathematicians? A lot of maths papers are written in German."

Joan said "So you studied mathematics with a bit of languages, Cooper?

Ron explained "Oh yes, but actually maths covers a huge range of subjects. The branch of mathematics I was most interested in was cryptology – you know codes and that sort of thing."

Joan was impressed. "So, we have a Welsh, German and French speaking mathematical person with an interest in codes running the Administration of a front-line RAF station – and popular with the new boss."

Ron made a modest response. "Jack of all trades and master of none. My job here is to keep things running smoothly so bomber command can fulfil its role. You know "strike sure strike hard" as it says on the coat of arms. To me that mostly means getting everything the boys need – they are doing the really tough and courageous bit – we're just a sideshow."

Joan made a change of subject "What did you tell Group Captain Ryland about his nephew? Whatever it was he was pleased in a sad sort of way. He seemed convinced you have done a good job on something."

Ron was puzzled "Sorry, ma'am, not with you. I never met Group Captain Ryland before yesterday, let alone his nephew."

They were at the door of the hanger. Ron held the iron framed pedestrian side door open for Joan. "Here we are."

Joan said "His nephew was Peter Jamieson – his sister's boy – he used to be based here."

Ron was amazed and looked it. "I didn't know that."

The inside of the maintenance hanger looked different every time Ron had been there. Sometimes it was a cavernous empty space; sometimes jam packed with aircraft in various states of repair or of disrepair. Today, the main show was a Lancaster bomber with a huge crane looming over it with the upper centre turret being lifted out, or being put back, Ron couldn't tell. The aircraft carried the letter 'WS' – Whisky Sugar, which sounded to Ron like a good concoction for a cure for colds. Various technicians were beavering away, led by Leading Mechanic Charge-hand 'Bill' Sykes. Bill was a large bluff looking man with a ruddy complexion, for whom the workers under him had huge respect. It did not do to get onto the wrong side of an argument with Bill Sykes, who could be quite robust in his verbal delivery.

Joan took in the scene as she looked round the hanger. "There's a lot of equipment in here – do you have problems getting anything?"

Ron nodded "All the time, but you get to know the wrinkles after a while. By and large we do ok." He knew Joan had come to see the WAAFs. He pointed to the far side of the hanger where there were some internal offices constructed inside the huge building. “The WAAFS work from the offices in the corner, over there.”

Joan seemed to have lost some formality in the walk to the hanger. “Thanks, no doubt I will see you around Cooper. You seem to be everywhere.”

He called after her “Glad to help Ma’am. I’ve got to catch up with the Charge Hand.” Ron turned to walk over to Bill Sykes and his team of busy bees.

He saw Ron coming “Morning Sarge. Have you come to see about my turret for Whisky Sugar?”

Ron knew they were going to be after some bits to put the Lancaster back in the air, but they were still at the diagnostic stage. He answered with another question “Yes. What’s the score?”

Sykes said “Well it’s a bit of a bugger. They took some flack and a bit started a small fire near the turret rotating mechanism. They managed to put the fire out, luckily without anyone getting seriously hurt and the whole air frame looks quite undamaged.”

Ron looked at the list he had in his hand from the message that his team had taken earlier on. “So we just need to get a new bearing housing and mounting?”

Sykes scratched his head. “Not as easy as all that. Although it looks ok, there is some distortion to either the frame just around the turret, or the turret itself, or both. We’ll have to get it all out and measure up. Could be a big job. Although the old girl’s quite airworthy, we could end up replacing huge chunks of the mainframe to get the turret serviceable.”

Ron asked "So the rest of the aircraft is ok?"

He received a "Yup" from Sykes.

After a second or two Ron mused "Would it fly without a turret?"

Bill Sykes looked sideways "Not sure what you mean, Sarge. You'd have to sheet the hole in and the thing would have to be trimmed differently, I suppose it would be nose heavy. Were you thinking of flying it back to the works? They've certainly got better jigs than us – we are just a front line workshop. It would take weeks to get it through their system though, I bet.

Ron said "In the meantime we are down by one Lanc."

Sykes said "I need to talk to Ops and the Engineering Officer, we might cannibalise it for bits."

Ron raised his hand in a sort of 'Wait a minute' gesture. He said "I've got different ideas; I might talk to the old man."

Sykes looked askance "You are always trying to fix things through a back door. You don't mean Ryland?"

Ron nodded "Yes, we seem to get on ok."

Sykes put his hands on his hips "You've got ideas above your station. Still I'll let you know when we've finished measuring up."

✝

Ten days had gone by after Group Captain Ryland's arrival at Whittingsmore, when he summoned Sergeant Ron Cooper to a meeting. Ryland was intrigued about Cooper. The chap seemed to have so many facets to his character and from a check on his personnel file, the RAF had, by and large, ignored his capabilities so far. Ron entered Ryland's office with a little trepidation.

"So Cooper, you wanted to see me? Something about statistics. You'd better keep it simple, I'm no boffin – although looking at your file, I think you might be."

Ron started "Sir, I have an idea from looking at the stats – the statistics from the raids."

Ryland said "Shouldn't you be looking after the station, not delving into ops? Anyway, ops info is classified, how do you know about it?"

Ron thought this might be the tricky bit "I don't Sir – well I do in one way. All the losses, personnel and equipment, come through me and any parts for repairs and so on. They are all listed here in the files." Ron had with him an envelope containing a summary of weather conditions and losses of equipment.

"Go on." said Ryland with an expression that was hard to read.

Ron proceeded. "These are the weather reports. I've used some mathematical tricks to correlate – to tie up – the two sets of figures – the weather reports and the losses I mean."

Ryland thought that this was getting interesting "Losses due to bad weather you mean, I take it?"

Ron replied "No Sir, I mean enemy action. We had significantly less battle damage on the dates marked here" He had the figures and tables out and was pointing to specific records. Without waiting for a reaction he said "And I know the reason."

Ryland leaned forward "This sounds interesting."

Ron explained "It's the tail wind – or a lack of head wind. A tail wind out, followed by a tail wind back improves survivability considerably. It's the speed over the ground you see. Even a small increase in speed makes a big difference to the enemy. They don't have time to alert the ack-ack but particularly to scramble the fighters."

Ryland asked "How did you work that out?"

"One of my gals worked in our Air Defence Operations Room, Sir. It takes time to track, identify, and decide whether to get fighters scrambled. It will be the same for the Jerries, although they have defences in depth."

Ryland wasn't sure what Cooper was getting at, "Catch'em by surprise you mean? I see. Still we can't control the weather – if only we could. An interesting academic exercise Cooper, but is that all?"

Ron said "We could make the bombers faster."

Ryland liked to keep an open mind but he could see where the conversation was going "Just like that? If only it was that easy. Look, we have got fast light bombers, you know, the Mosquitoes. But they are light. Can't get a big bomb load in them."

Ron now put his proposal "Sir, if I may, I think we have here a solution. In Hanger 2 there's a Lanc. It's laid up. It's turned out to be a big job to fix the upper centre turret. If we took the turret out and sheeted over the hole, it would be less weight and more speed."

"What!" exclaimed Ryland.

Ron summarised "Sir, I calculate, from theory, it would be about twenty knots quicker. If there are no fighters in the sky why do we need guns?" Was this going to be the point at which he was booted out of the office?

Ryland picked up the sheet of paper and walked over to the window, studying the figures. Ron kept quiet.

After a long silence he said "Sounds crazy, but thinking the unthinkable – sometimes it pays off. That's all Cooper and thanks."

As Ron left he heard Ryland picking up the phone. "Polly, is Squadron Leader Askew in his hut?"

Later that day, Simon Askew was in the office of the CO. He ventured his opinion of the scheme that was being suggested. "It's bonkers Sir. The upper turret is the one that gets the most fighters. We'd be leaving our top exposed."

Ryland however appeared to be seized with enthusiasm for the idea. "Why don't we try it? We've got a Lanc out of action in Hanger 2. We could use it on a specific raid. Let's just try it. Have a go. Get the thing modified and just try it a couple of times, if it looks dodgy then we'll can it. I'll talk to the chaps."

Askew knew he was going to have to go along with it. Maybe it was worth a try but it did seem contrary to common sense and his experience of brushes with enemy fighters. "Ok Sir, you're the boss. But I'll fly it myself, I couldn't ask the boys to take the risk."

Chapter 3

There were occasional opportunities for socialising both on and off the Bomber Command station. Dances seemed to be held on an irregular basis rather than to any fixed timetable. There were always new RAF people about with the ebb and flow of service postings. These events had a downside, which everyone tried not to notice. There were a significant number of aircrew who didn't come back from missions, but somehow everyone managed to put it to the back of their mind. It was the only way to go on. The dances were supplemented by the presence of locals from the nearby civilian communities.

Ron and Bob Neal were propping up the bar and taking more interest in the beer than the dancing, although Ron liked the current fashion in music. The band that had been cobbled together was pretty competent and had picked up the tunes that were all the rage. As the Tenor Sax launched into an improvisation set in 'String of Pearls', Ron thought they were particularly good at this one. There was a good contingent of uniformed and civilian bodies cavorting about the floor. Ron sipped his beer and tapped his feet, but Ron did not do dancing – it was not his thing.

Bob quaffed his drink "It's a good pint Ron. They seemed to have found out how to keep it."

Ron smiled "Just watch how many you have. We don't want a hangover from the beer, making for heavy weather with your weather forecasts!"

Bob enjoyed his beer "A couple of pints will improve my reading of the charts I assure you." He nodded towards the twirling figures progressing round the dance floor. "I see that blonde Section Officer is out there with Askew. She's a bit tasty isn't she?"

Ron had had to agree "Definitely easy on the eye." Joan was dancing with Askew and as the duo passed the corner of the bar she made eye contact with Ron over Askew's shoulder. She smiled and Ron nodded an acknowledgment.

Bob seemed to notice more in the gesture than Ron did. "If you ask me you might stand a bit of a chance there. She might be dancing with Askew, but she keeps looking your way."

Ron's face formed an untypically blank expression. "I'm not with you, I hadn't noticed anything."

Bob shook his head in bewilderment. "For a man who seems to know everything that's going on, you don't seem to know much here. I'm telling you, you ought to go and have a dance with her."

Ron stoically returned to his beer. "Well, two things to think about there. Officers should be dancing with Officers surely. You can't mix the Sergeants with the Commissioned ranks, although I agree we let them mix together to fly aeroplanes and even have breakfast together afterwards. The other thing is I can't dance."

Bob was never happier than when giving advice. "Well I don't think she's as stuffy as she makes out, and anyway, none of us blokes can dance properly. Have another beer, you'll think you can dance properly after that."

Ron turned to attract the bar steward's attention, absent mindedly scanning the stock behind the bar. "Thanks for the advice but I think I'll stick by the bar. When are you next on duty?"

Ron had not noticed that Joan had completed her dance and she had sidled up to the bar behind him. Ron continued to talk to Bob without looking in his direction as he tried to attract the bar stewards attention. "I'll buy you another as long as you've got time to recover."

Ron was startled to hear Joan voice. "Are you buying the drinks Sergeant Cooper?" He had thought she was on the other side of the room, not right behind him.

Ron stammered "Ah, Ma'am, ah, yes, ah, I was, eh, just buying the drinks, yes, can I get you something?"

Joan responded straightway "I'll just have a small shandy, please."

Bob jumped in "Mine's a pint, Ron."

Joan asked "So, what were you two talking about? You looked as if you were putting the world to rights."

Ron was not sure what he had been saying but Bob answered for him "We were talking about the weather Ma'am. " He drained the dregs from his glass. "What else would you expect a meteorologist to talk about?"

Joan tossed her head back and smiled "Do all the Sergeants make strange remarks at this base?"

Bob chuckled defensively "I'd better go before I put my foot in it anymore. He passed Joan her drink while Ron paid. "Cheers Ron" He picked up his fresh pint and with an "Excuse me Ma'am," drifted off in no general direction.

Joan said, "Well Sergeant Cooper, perhaps you should teach me a bit of Welsh, or should it be German? And thanks for the drink by the way."

Ron had recovered his composure from the surprise of being out flanked by a pretty, but senior, officer. Ron felt more ready for a verbal joust. "French, you didn't mention French. Mind you I'm not so hot on French these days."

Joan gave a provocative look over the rim of her glass, which Ron noticed was already stained with her red lipstick. "I might be hot on French myself."

Ron was beginning to think Bob was right. He raised his eyebrows "Really, really?"

*

Weeks went by at Whittingsmoor with losses that Ron thought were variable in the deteriorating autumn weather, but he was not now so close to the figures. He could not avoid seeing all sorts of data in his support role but he had decided to keep clear of the operations activities. And – to be seen to do so. He had made a bit of a gamble with his suggestion to Ryland a few weeks previously, which he thought at the time had gone ok. He knew they had been up to something with Whisky Sugar and suspected that it had been flown in the hours of darkness, but wise discretion had prevailed over curiosity.

However, he took onboard the comments from the Group Captain that implied he had been prying into ops – which could be construed as an unhealthy interest in matters classified. Here he now was, back outside the CO's office straightening his forage cap. Had he put his foot in it? The telephone rang on the desk of the CO's secretary.

"You're to go in" said Polly, after she put the phone down.

Ryland said "Ah, Cooper."

Ron did his best 'at attention' impression. "You wanted to see me Sir."

Ryland said "Yes. I wanted to let you know various pieces of news. An update you might say. At ease. Have a seat."

A wave of relief swept over Ron. This did not seem like a dressing down. On the contrary, it was positively cordial. "Thank you Sir."

Ryland began "Firstly, you may know that we tried the Lanc, Whisky Sugar, without its upper turret. Souped her up a bit, polished the skin and what-not too. Got nearly another 40 knots out of her."

Ron stayed silent but noted that it was a greater improvement than he had estimated originally.

Ryland went on "Took her out three times, on her own, or with Mosquitoes, fast raids in small groups just over the French and Belgian coast. Seems to me your theory was correct. They never saw an interceptor and even problems with flak were reduced. The closest a fighter got was within about half a mile of their tail, just before they crossed the Channel on the way back. Seems to me your theory was correct."

Ron felt satisfied and vindicated. "That is good news Sir."

Ryland said "Well I thought so. In fact I put it upstairs to the Brass at Command. Frankly, it wasn't well received. Two reasons – mostly they thought it bad for morale – the brave gunner protecting his mates and all that. Even though the boys here are a bit more convinced now than they were."

Ron had wanted to be careful that his pleasure at the outcome did not seem smug, but here was the negative side – the RAF hierarchy was not receptive. On the other hand, the crews presumably thought him less barmy now than at the beginning. "Sir, but surely the low loss rate – well lack of losses, fits with the maths – the statistical predictions?"

Ryland was obviously being quite open "The top men said there were not enough raids to justify that as a finding – to see a trend – but in any case, it was probably the smaller groups that made the difference. The thinking was that Jerry was ignoring them as they knew a small group couldn't do much damage. Anyway they've canned the first and last turretless Lanc. We'll stick Whisky Sugar in the back of the hanger while we decide what to do with her. You had a good idea Cooper and I appreciate it.

It seemed that was that. Ron started to rise "Will that be all Sir?

Ryland waved him back down. "Sit down Cooper, there's more, lots more. What I'm about to tell you is classified to the highest level – Most Secret. We need to accommodate a special unit on the Station with access to the aerodrome but fenced off, no prying eyes. We need a biggish hanger.

Here was another project, thought Ron. It sounded interesting. "I've got you Sir. The hanger in the north corner has dispersal stores in there. It's where the old road used to cross the aerodrome. None of the locals go near it since the road was cut by the construction of the air field, years ago.

"Good." said Ryland "The Unit will arrive in the next couple of days. I think they will fly some aircraft in too. One or maybe two. I want you to be the Liaison Officer between us, the RAF and this Unit.

Ron was a bit surprised at the form of his words "Liaison Officer? ...Sir?"

Ryland came out with a bombshell. "That's the other thing. As of now you have been commissioned Flight Lieutenant."

Ron's mind raced. Had he misheard? Misunderstood? He was currently a sergeant and Flight Lieutenant was a huge leap into the commissioned ranks. How could this be possible? All he could say was "Sir!"

Ryland made a 'calm down' gesture with his hands "Yes, yes. Any number of reasons. I think you should have had a commission when you first joined. You've skipped some ranks – unusual, but these are unusual circumstances. You're clever, Cooper and we need your brains. The Special Unit, they're called SOE (A) by the way, have stuff that is classified 'Officers Only'. So we wouldn't want that getting in the way would we?" He raised a finger and tapped the side of his nose.

Ron's composure was shot, but he tried to ask a sensible question. "What about the rest of my responsibilities, Sir?"

Ryland replied "We need to find you an assistant, I still want the Station to run smoothly. Think of the SOE Area as a base within a base."

Ron had never heard of SOE or SOE(A) "SOE, Sir?"

Ryland said "I gather it stands for Special Operations Executive with an A at the end indicating Air Operations. God knows what they do, it's not part of the RAF. It seems to have bits and pieces of all the forces, but is controlled from the top, and I mean the top. My orders were signed WSC. So put that in your pipe and smoke it!"

This was turning into some day. Ron checked out what he was thinking “Churchill you mean Sir?”

“Yes.” said Ryland. “There’s another thing – anything you want, you get. That’s another reason for your rank. Use as much discretion as possible – we want it to be unnoticed, but if anyone obstructs you come straight to me. Now go and organise getting that hanger cleared out. We’ll need some offices inside the hanger. It’s got to be self contained and as invisible as we can make it. You will need to tell a few of the team of course, but strictly on a need to know basis. We’ve got a week or so. I expect you can get yourself a new uniform in that time!”

Chapter 4

It was a cold damp fog that enfolded RAF Whittingsmore, made more unpleasant since the fog was drifting on a slight air movement that added to the chill. Perhaps the fog was clearing, thought Ron. It had been still air and thick fog for a couple of days, but now it was swirling a little and every now and then visibility improved before the mist closed in again. The dark shadow of a hangar was visible nearby where four men were loading up a variety of non-perishable stores into an RAF lorry parked in front of the hangar doors. There were crates and boxes, mostly containing spares, some large frames that were probably something to do with aircraft maintenance and the odd recognisable items such as bits of office furniture. The men were working under Ron's instructions, clearing a space in the hangar. One of the men was Rhys Evans. Rhys had been on this job before; although then he was moving stuff into the spare hangar for dispersal purposes.

As ever, Ron was muffled against the damp and cold, but now a Flight Lieutenant's cap covered his head somewhat more completely than the perfunctory cover of the forage cap he used to have. Under his greatcoat was the rest of a commissioned officer's uniform that he was still getting used to. The enlisted men had duffle jackets as well as overalls, even though they were working – lifting and carrying. The exception was Rhys who just had overalls and never seemed bothered by cold, damp weather. They were just about finished loading up.

As he passed Ron, who was checking items on a clipboard, Rhys said in Welsh *"Beth yw hyn i gyd am Sarge? Does dim ond wech wythnos ddar i ni ei gosod mewn yma."*[4]

Ron responded in English. "A few points". Lowering his clip board to his side, Ron gestured with his pencil. "One. I've not spent all this time helping you with English for you to speak Welsh on duty. Two, I can't get used to the idea, but you've got to call me Sir. It's the way the RAF works. And finally no questions – just get on with it.

"Yes sir!" said Rhys as he put the last box in the lorry "It's all done now."

Ron smiled, but then his expression changed as he put his head on one side. He looked up towards the sky through the slightly shifting mist. "Can you hear an aircraft?

Rhys scanned the sky. The odd patch of blue kept appearing and disappearing. "Yes Sir. Sounds like it's circling above the fog. There, look." He pointed, as momentarily a shape could almost be made out. "No...... it's gone."

An aircraft movement in these conditions, and in the middle of the day, was unexpected. Two days ago, Ops brought some bombers back in a very foggy dawn but only just got them down by the use of FIDO. Everyone called it FIDO which as far as Ron could remember stood for 'Fog – Intensive Dispersal Operation'. This was a system comprising a network of pipes that supplied petrol to the edges of the runway. When the petrol was ignited, the heat temporarily dispersed the fog, but it used an immense amount of precious fuel and the effect didn't last long.

---

4 *"What's all this about Sarge? It's only six weeks since we put it in here."*

A return from a raid was a planned movement event; evidently whatever was going up in the sky now was not.

The sound of the aircraft was distinctive – whatever it was had a Merlin engine or engines. An evocative sound, which today was muffled by fog and distance. On this occasion it was also overlayed with a stuttering sound typical of an engine in trouble. Ron said "It's not one of theirs." The sound receded, but then they could tell it was coming round for an approach. "Crikey he's having a go at landing. This is going to be a bit dicey."

More and more clear patches had been appearing in the fog over the last few minutes. Then the engine note of the mystery aircraft rose, then fell, then rose again. There was the sound of tyres on concrete heard through the fog. Bursting through a patch of mist they saw an aircraft on the runway a few hundred yards in front of them. Only one engine was turning. A wheel left the edge of the hardened runway and dropped into the softer grassed area, causing the aeroplane to swing off the runway and onto a collision course with a pill box at the edge of the field. Ron and Rhys stood rooted to the spot. In apparent slow motion they watched in horror, as despite its slackening speed, it smacked into the pill box. Clods of earth and grass were thrown up into the air during its passage which now fell back to earth. The whole thing has only taken a second or two but it seemed like minutes. It could now be seen that the aircraft was a twin engined Mosquito. The port engine had hit the pill box. A huge gouge in the grass traced the path of the Mosquito to where it now rested in silence save for some creaking noise. The remaining engine had stopped when it hit the ground.

Rhys was already running towards the spot where the stricken aeroplane lay. Ron started after him, then in a moment of coolness realised that an instant reaction might not be the best. He stopped and shouted after the receding figure of Rhys "Watch yourself Evans!" The other men started to come back out of the hangar.

Ron realised the best outfit to deal with this were the guys of the crash team. However, unlike where a mission was returning or other routine landings, they would not be on standby. He said to the men who had just emerged from the hangar and who looked a bit uncertain, “Catch Evans and stop him doing anything daft. I’ll call the rescue team.” In the fog there was no guarantee that the crash team had been alterted by the sound of the impact. There was a telephone in a hood on the outside of the hangar.

After making the calls Ron ran back towards the wreck. Rhys was jumping down from the cockpit. Evidently the other men had failed to catch Rhys to stop him climbing on the wreck. The pilot was half out of a smashed window. From both the posture of the pilot and the body language and appearance of Rhys, Ron could guess the news was not good. Ron panted out “You’re covered in blood Rhys. My God, what a mess.”

Rhys too was out of breath. “No navigator on board – just the pilot – and I’m afraid he’s dead, Sir.”

Ron decided that it was best for them all to retire to a safe distance and await the rescue team. Nobody wanted to be incinerated in a fireball that often followed a crash.

Ron and his team retreated towards the hangar and then sat sullenly on the tailboard of the truck. They watched the crash crew through the clearing mist. They were well practiced and no fire to deal with this time. A stretcher was loaded into an ambulance and one of the crash team came over and showed Ron a dog tag taken from the pilot.

Ron asked “The aircraft looks okay – how come he copped it?”

The man replied “It happens Sir. Looks to me that he hit his head on something. His seat belts were off. My guess is he took his belts off to peer through the fog looking for somewhere to land.”

Ron said “He’s not from this base. I’ll find out who he is.”

Ron and the team closed up the truck and returned to the mess in silence.

Later that day Rhys and Ron were having a debrief in the Orderly Room. Ron had kept his office there, which was still better than the rooms that most other Officers had.

Sally came in. “I’ve tracked down the base where the crashed Mossie came from Sir. It’s from an experimental wing. They want to talk to you.”

Ron said “Get them on the blower.” He turned to Rhys “Bit of a shake-up eh Evans? Suddenly seems a bit cosy and isolated here in the backroom.”

Rhys shrugged “I’ve worked with the undertakers a bit at home. Saw a few bodies there. It was more… “ He said something in Welsh then reverted to English “what’s the word …… shocking….. the first time.”

The phone rang and Ron answered. Rhys heard Ron’s end of the conversation “Hello, yes that’s me. …. Yes, he bought it I’m afraid. …. Yes. ….. No. ….. Usual channels for aircrew. Yes. …. Our team here will do that. …… No idea yet. Yes, we’ll let you know – maybe tomorrow night.” Ron put the phone down.

Rhys enquired “Anything you need doing, Sir?”

Ron said “The usual that Ops do with the deceased. Let his CO know. Sally has all the details, she’ll do that. But find a tarpaulin and cover up the wreck. We need to get someone to find out how bad the damage is. Even though the pilot was killed, the aircraft itself didn’t look too bad.”

Sally came back in. "Group Captain Ryland wants you over at the north hangar to meet some people, sir. Wouldn't say who."

"What? Now? It's all happening at once." Ron had almost forgotten about the expected new arrivals. "That will be our new colleagues – let's call them the North Team." Ron put his cap and coat on and left the office.

"North Team?" said Sally. "What's that mean? Bit cloak and dagger."

Rhys waxed lyrical "Ours is not to reason why. That's Tennyson that is."

Sally riposted "My, my – English literature as well as language now."

*

Ryland's car had picked up Ron at the door to the orderly room, but Ron was slightly startled to find Ryland himself was the driver. No doubt a measure to limit the number of people at close quarters and seeing what might be going on. Ryland drove across the aerodrome to the North Hangar on the far side from most of the buildings of the air base. The fog had cleared and the sun was making intermittent appearances. "It's brightening up." said Ryland as he pulled up. "Let's take the air." Ron and Ryland got out of the staff car and walked to the main doors of the hangar. The doors could be rolled back enough to let aircraft in and out, but Ron had arranged for them to be left slid open about 15 feet apart. It was enough to drive a lorry straight in. Ryland had a brief look into the hangar, not going more than about 20 feet inside. Apparently satisfied, he then turned and walked back to the outside. Taking up a position on the outside corner of the hangar he looked back over the airfield and round about him. There were no other people in sight over on this side.

For a second or two they stood silently taking in the calm of the scene. It was an unexpected quiet space that contrasted with the usual hectic routine. There were birds singing and a slight ticking and creaking from metal walls of the hangar as it responded to the sunshine warming the face of the building. "Looks like we have got here before our visitors."

Ron had no idea from which direction the 'vistors' from SOE (A) would be travelling to Whittingsmore, but they would be coming an indirect route once they got closer to the airfield. The main gatehouse entrance was convenient from most places, accessed readily from the main road network and the road that led to the railway station – that was why the main entrance was where it was. To reach a point on the north side would usually entail driving a round about route of some distance unless you had access within the perimeter. There was a patchwork of small country lanes round the base, two of which had been severed by the construction of the airfield. Villages that had been close to one another in 1930 were now miles apart by a forced diversion. There was an ancillary gate in the perimeter fence, formed of wire mesh on an iron frame, where one of those lanes had formerly crossed the area at a point next to the North Hangar. The gate merged into the run of the perimeter fence when viewed from anything other than close up. The presence of the old road surface under the gate gave away its former use – there were still some road markings visible.

The gate was kept padlocked. Ron had the key in his pocket, as this was the gate agreed as the access for the Special Operations team, for reason of discretion. They could avoid the gatehouse and main thoroughfares. Ron had made sure the lock was not rusted up on the previous day. He didn't want the embarrassment of not being able to get it open in front of the CO and the new arrivals. Ron and Ryland walked over to the gate and looked through the mesh down the unused road. The hedges and verges had encroached from each side and grown higher – it would be difficult to notice comings and goings from most places. They could only see about 50 or 60 yards of the old road, but they could hear a car approaching. Ron unlocked the padlock and swung open the gate. Ryland said "Let's put them straight in the hangar." He wanted the small convoy in the open for as short a time as possible to minimise rumours on the base.

There were in fact, two cars and a lorry. The leading car pulled up opposite Ron and Ryland. A man of about thirty, dressed in civilian clothes was in the front passenger seat. He rolled down the window "You must be Group Captain Ryland and Flight Lieutenant Cooper?"

Ryland said "Yes, that's right."

The occupant of the car thrust out an ID card "I'm Nicholson" and passed another piece of paper to Ryland. Ron wondered whether they were supposed to give some password, but as they hadn't been briefed to expect one, they wouldn't know what it should have been. Funny, thought Ron, a Group Captain acting as gate guard and less security here than you would get normally.

Ryland pointed to the open hangar "Thanks, we'll do the formalities inside. Drive in there."

Ron waved all three vehicles towards the hangar and went back to re-lock the gate. Ryland briskly strode the few paces behind the lorry and into the large open space within the hangar that now held two cars and a lorry. When Ron caught up and turned into the hangar he saw Nicholson open the door, get out and shake Ryland's hand. Ryland returned the ID but tucked the paper into his tunic pocket. Other men got out of cars, all in civilian clothes. There wasn't any saluting going on, but then civilians didn't salute or get saluted and who knew what the rank situation might be anyhow. One thing that was clear was that Nicholson was in charge.

Ron joined Ryland and Nicholson. Ryland was talking. "Cooper has sorted this spot out for you. We hope it's discreet enough." There were six men and the driver of the lorry. There was a flurry of introductions which Ron quickly forgot.

Ron showed the assembled men the offices within the buildings. These were constructed of part glazed partition walls that were positioned against the sides of the hangar. "We have power, phones, and the offices have stove heaters. I guess this hangar space is big enough for maybe three small aircraft. We were using it as a dispersal store. Will you be wanting to keep aircraft in here? We normally only keep the ones under repair in hangars."

Nicholson ignored the question as they drew chairs round a table in an office that was set up as a meeting room.

Nicholson was business-like, but friendly. "You know how hush-hush all this is don't you? It stands repeating."

Ryland was reassuring "We've all been briefed. Cooper here will be your liaison officer. He has full authority to get anything you need."

Nicholson gestured towards the lorry through the glass wall of the office "We've brought a lot with us." He chuckled slightly, "We try to be self contained. We also get a lot of stuff by unusual channels. We don't like too many people knowing what we've got and what we're doing with it".

There was a short discussion about billets, access and provisions. A meeting was set up for the following day when it was agreed Ron would return for a full briefing. Ryland drove them back to the main part of the base. "Get yourself a car Cooper. You will need it to go back and forth."

Ron kept quiet. Driving, now there's a thing. Ron had not driven since University days. His uncle had a farm and kept an old car in a barn which was only used occasionally. Ron had practiced with the car, a tiny Humber Chummy. Although this had helped Ron get a licence he had never passed a test. Still, for the time being it looked like he could just use an RAF car to drive across the base without going on the public road. He would manage.

*

Ron returned to the north hangar the next day to find the SOE(A) team all settled in. There were quite a few bits and pieces stashed around the various offices – lots of filing cabinets and electrical equipment of sorts. Ron glanced at it.

Nicholson came in and saw the direction of Ron's casual gaze. "It's a radio. Can you get us a mast to stick up an aerial?"

"Of course. How soon? You'll need to tell me exactly what's required."

Nicholson was reassuring. "Thanks – we'll let you have a note of what we need. Now, then. Sit down, it's Ron isn't it. We work on first names here – we're not a stuffy bunch and we are a mixture of RAF, Army and civilians. It's going to take a while to get you up to speed. But that starts now. Let's go over what we are doing. We are, you might say, an unconventional team. Frankly, we are fighting a dirty war. The other side don't play cricket and we need to tell you stuff that will make your hair curl and turn your stomach. It's difficult to know where to start, but our job is to kill Germans."

Ron thought to himself, I suppose that's what we all do in Bomber Command – in the war – that is what we are all doing. But put like that it seemed a bit well, direct, and a bit personal. He vocalised his thoughts "I like to think we're trying to win a war, but I suppose we know we must kill lots of Germans on any bomber raid."

"The difference is – we have a list."

Ron hesitated. "A list….."

"Yes, a list of 53 Nazis which we think are key to undermining the enemy. If they were eliminated the war might not be won but the balance would change."

Ron thought he had got the idea straightaway. "Interesting. So people like Hitler, Goering, Goebbels and so on would be at the top I suppose."

Nicholson went on "Well yes, that seems obvious and indeed they are on the list, but it's been thought about more deeply than that. Some of the top Nazis might not be that good as military leaders, and by eliminating them we might risk promoting someone with real talent – although it does seem that anyone capable, is more of a professional military man and less of a Nazi party person."

Ron thought 'So the list would contain who? Less high-profile leaders? Middle ranking generals?'

The brief continued "The top Nazis, Hitler and his coterie and so on are there, but it's a matter of target priority. The big names are well protected, and difficult to find – especially since the Heydrich business."

Heydrich was a leading Nazi who had been appointed as the Nazi Governor of occupied Czechoslovakia. Ron knew that Czech patriots had assassinated Heydrich in an attack.

"Would it surprise you to learn that we, SOE, trained them in England and sent them out there, with arms we provided?"

Nicholson looked for a reaction in the thoughtful face of the Flight Lieutenant he had only just met the day before. There was surprise in that expression, yes – but something else – curiosity probably. “It was a successful attack in one way. A nasty high profile Nazi in an occupied country was done for. But the Nazis took huge and vicious reprisals against men, women and children from villages who they thought might be connected with the resistance fighters. Collective punishment to deter others. Like I say, they don’t play cricket.”

Ron was assimilating this information. He spoke in a reflective way "I suppose we kill civilians every night in the towns we bomb, but I don’t know, it is somehow different. Still……”

“Yes, maybe – maybe not. Our job is not to moralise, but let’s get back to the list. There are four reasons to be on the list. High profile party man, anyone effective militarily and technical people. There are a few engineers and scientists on their side we would like to see removed from the picture.”

“I can see that – the Germans have got pretty good kit from what I have seen and heard.” Ron knew there was always both pride and concern among crews about keeping a technical advantage in the equipment they had. At Whittingsmoor they were fortunate that they had the latest aeroplanes – Lancasters and a few Mosquitoes. RAF crews were always being posted to different outfits and the stories from air crew suggested that some British aircraft were not always top drawer. There was also dependence on the technical kit, like radios and whatever other stuff was involved operationally. What it all did, Ron did not know, but secret electrical equipment was being added all the time to RAF bombers. Then there was the opposite concern about what the other lot had. Not much was said, in case it was criticised for having had a morale sapping tone. But it was to Ron’s direct knowledge from his university days, that German engineers and scientists were very capable.

So, senior Nazis, Military men and technical people – that left one other group. "Who makes up the fourth lot?"

Nicholson drew a breath and let out a sigh. "The German Reich has decided to eliminate anyone who doesn't fit their racial ideals. Jews in particular, but there are horrific stories coming back of wholesale deportations, murder. Hitler has also said irregular forces like commandos will get the same fate. Political opponents, religious groups and so on are all getting put in slave labour concentration camps and being systematically and horribly murdered, mostly by starvation and working to death. Some other racial groups as well, but the one that is closest to home are resistance workers in the occupied countries – we have close associations with them and many have been victims. Frankly, there is the personal element for us – these are people we know."

"Phew. This all takes some thinking about." Ron had heard talk about stuff like this, but now had to confront it. One thing though, it made you even more sure you were on the right side.

"It's not just vengeance, although it is a part of it under the surface I suppose" remarked Nicholson. "We need to disrupt the Gestapo and SS terror network if we can. It would help morale in the occupied countries amongst the resistance. That's what the Heydrich assassination was supposed to do, but the cost of the Nazi retaliation was not really reckoned with."

Suddenly Ron understood the thinking and that thinking defined the mission in hand. "So we have to bump off these goons without it looking like an assassination."

"Exactly. The objective of this organisation, SOE (Λ), is to arrange for the Bosch on the list to be 'accidentally' killed in an air raid."

Ron wondered how this could be done. "That's a tall order – impossible surely."

"Well, we have some ideas, but let's take a break." Having summarised the key parts of the briefing Nicholson came up with a change of subject. "What's the story with the crash yesterday?"

"Oh, you know about that? Word travels fast – it's supposed to be a bit sensitive. The squadron it came from……."

Ron was interrupted by Nicholson "You're involved with a very funny team now. We can find out whatever we want, more or less. Anyway your crashed Mosquito – it's from an experimental development unit, I think."

Ron was impressed. "So it seems. Why do you ask? Anyway what about security – this aeroplane is supposed to be classified. Where do we stand with that?"

"Classified? As you can see we can find out what we need if it is of interest. We just keep it in this team." Nicholson gave an intriguing look. "We are just having some thoughts …… and I think your crashed Mossie might be of interest. "What did the experimental unit tell you and more important, what did you tell them?"

"I said it was pranged but wasn't sure of a full damage report. To be honest I talked more about the pilot – poor blighter. I said it had hit the pillbox. They said to cover it up until they could sort something out. "

They had a tea break and Ron went into another office and made a couple of calls – one to Ryland and the other to the CO of the experimental wing. If they were going to poke around in a classified project from another outfit he wanted his backside covered. From the response to the calls it seemed his new colleagues did have clout – the usual RAF palaver seemed to get sidestepped. When Ron returned to the meeting room Nicholson had been joined by one or two of the SOE men they had met the previous day. One of them was Frank Nash. "Ron, this is Frank Nash. Frank is our equipment officer, a sort of gadget man. Frank, meet Ron Cooper." Over the tea it became apparent that the crashed Mossie situation had been the attention of the SOE(A) team who had done some overnight homework. "We think that we might be able to do something with the wrecked Mosquito. We'd like to go and have a look at it when we have finished our tea."

Twenty minutes later, Ron, Nicholson and Nash had left the hangar and had walked the short distance to the crash site. Various bits of tarpaulin covered the nose and cockpit of the aircraft, in a rushed overnight cover-up job. The tail was sticking up exposed. Nash had donned a siren suit.

Frank Nash wasted no time it getting under the tarp and he had brought a small trenching spade. He did a bit of fiddling about under the nose where it was gouged into the ground.

He came out muddied and panting as he drew himself upright again. "Yes, as we thought – it has got it. We should get it inside. Can you fix that up Ron? Make sure the minimum number of people are used and keep the nose covered up."

What did 'it has got it' mean? Ron seemed to be the only one not in the know. "Is there something special here?"

They started walking back towards the hangar. Nicholson replied smiling. "There is always something special for us. We'll explain more when we know ourselves. By the way, leave room for a Lysander – we will be flying one in tonight, after dark. I want to keep it in there too."

Ron kept the questions coming. No doubt they would tell him when it went beyond the pail. “But Lysanders are slow artillery spotter planes aren’t they? Are you planning an artillery assault as well?

Nicholson laughed “No. … Well, maybe in a way. But no. The Lysander is really useful for our taxi service to the occupied countries. It will land on a sixpence. Agents and resistance people need transport.”

“Okay. We’ll leave room for your “taxi” and I’ll let the control tower know it’s coming. What time?”

“About 1900. See you tomorrow. We need to talk more when you have made all arrangements to get these two aeroplanes in our hangar”

Ron left to do just that. Maybe there would be more answers tomorrow.

Chapter 5

Dieter Fischer watched from his lofty position as dawn broke over the English countryside. The sun was behind him as he piloted his Bf110 photo reconnaissance aircraft heading almost due west, towards the central belt of England. His crew man Rolf Huber, seated behind him in the rear facing seat with a machine gun, could see the sun rising over the North Sea. It was going to be a clear cold day. Soon they would be easily seen by any sharp eyed observer on the ground, but for the moment they would be lost in the glare of the rising sun. Dieter Fischer had enjoyed his posting to the *Fernaufklärungsgruppe* photo reconnaissance squadron – it might be risky, but probably no more so than bombing runs over England. But on a mission like this Dieter was the master of his own destiny. He could pick his route, height and the order of the targets to be photographed by the forward facing cameras that had replaced the fighter bomber's canons. Their defence was not so much the single gun manned by Huber, but the fact that they were a lone aircraft travelling at speed and intending to stay away from hotly defended areas like cities and airfields.

Their mission was unusual. He was ordered to locate and photograph certain large country houses. One never questioned the object of a mission, but part of him wondered whether this was Hermann Goering optimistically window shopping for a splendid country residence in a conquered country. Such optimism would have looked less fanciful two years ago than it did now. He had been told to look out particularly for any sign of developments having been recently added to the historical buildings centred in these country estates. Some of these stately houses were quite easy to find from the air, due to the layout of avenues of trees and formal gardens that made distinctive patterns when viewed from altitude.

Having threaded their way across eastern England by making doglegs, avoiding the RAF bomber airfields, of which there now seemed to be many, they had crossed the Great North Road – a feature marked on their maps. They now progressed as far as Corby and Kettering, their position identified by the use of prominent landmarks, now lit up by the sun behind them. Coming from the east at this time of day and weaving through the bomber bases they could well have been detected, but hoped that they would be mis-identified by the English as a returning RAF bomber. The further west they went, the less effective this subterfuge would be, or so they assumed.

They intended to photograph three targets and return for home as fast as possible. By noting the position of some small bodies of water they found the first target. Holdenby House could be clearly identified from the main drive and the pattern of the landscaping around the house. Dieter tipped the nose towards the building and ran the cameras. It was so clear that they maintained a good attitude without risking going too low. The next target was a country house to the south of Rugby, near a village called Dunchurch. On this clear morning the railway lines radiating from the town of Rugby coordinated well with their map. The house was on a rise, clearly seen from the east. They photographed it from a height of 1000 meters and risked a return circuit at a lower height, again approaching from the east. They flew on without incident to the final target. This was harder to find.

Ashorne Hill was a country house southwest of Rugby and south of Coventry. Using visual references from the conurbations which they could clearly see in the distance, they headed towards the location. A clue was found in an unusual windmill matching their pre-flight briefing. The Chesterton windmill had a four-arched base and topped a low hill, but they still could not see the house, which should have been a kilometre to the west of the mill.

Dieter dropped the Bf110 to a lower altitude and flew a circuit, with both Huber and himself scanning the ground over the dipped wing as they made the turn. The house was well concealed in the woods, but then it flashed past below them. From the short glimpse, they could see there were roadways and extra accommodation huts having been built in the grounds of the estate. They would have to go lower to get good photographs – one more pass should do it. Dieter lined up the cameras, his thumb poised over the button on the control column, that in a different variant of the same aeroplane would fire the forward facing cannon. At that instant there were a series of cracks and bangs and the airframe shook. Dieter's guts tightened in response to an involuntary adrenalin rush. For a split second he was unsure what had happened, but then an acrid smell in the cockpit of hot metal and burned rubber hit his nostrils. Fluid was streaming from the starboard wing and with a sinking feeling he guessed they had been hit. Immediately this realisation dawned, there was a stream of tracer passing in front of the nose of the aircraft from above and behind. Dieter shouted to Huber, but getting no response he twisted his head round to see Huber slumped over his gun, a dark stain spreading over the shoulder of the observer's flying suit. Huber was grunting and groaning and evidently in a bad way. Through the cockpit canopy beyond Huber, flanking both sides of the aircraft – Spitfires! There were two RAF fighters in a menacing position, which almost as he saw the attackers, rattled off another stream of tracer, close to the Bf110.

Dieter quickly realised what had happened. In their concentration on the target, the British fighters had approached them from the sunward direction and opened fire before they were even spotted. What to do now? Dieter was trapped and at the mercy of his attackers. He was too low to bale out and this would not help Huber. Added to this, the controls were commanding his full attention as the aircraft became slightly unstable. One of the Spitfires pulled ahead and waggled its wings. Dieter knew this meant 'Follow me'. He had little choice.

*

The RAF Regiment squaddies in the guard room at Wellesbourne Mountford Aerodrome had never been called out so quickly. Within minutes, they joined crash tenders and an ambulance waiting at the side of the airstrip. A twin engined fighter-bomber of unfamiliar outline was being shepherded down the glide path, by two Spitfires. It made a tidy landing, its German markings clear now to the men on the ground. Almost before wheels had stopped it was surrounded by vehicles and the lead officer had his pistol trained on the pilot through the cockpit glass. He looked stunned and raised his hands.

Chapter 6

Ron Cooper was dividing his time between his 'old' job of administering RAF Whittingsmoor and his new role with the 'North Team'. Quite what his new job entailed was not clear yet, but his conversations with Ryland now centred on the business of the Orderly Room – mundane activities of base administration – with a 'by the way' discussion about the team in the north hangar. The day's discussion in Ryland's office followed a routine pattern. After looking through a report on level of stores, leave passes and personnel transfers, Ryland leaned back. "So, how is it going, Flight Lieutenant?"

Ron knew he meant the North Team. "They are an unusual bunch, sir."

Ryland made a sort of amused snort. "Yes, I know."

"Sir, I wanted to ask you about the crashed Mossie. It's in their hangar."

"Yes. They've done some deal with the high-ups over it. It's considered a write-off.

Ron raised his eybrows. "Oh really? I'm no expert, but it looks fixable to me. I could get Sykes to take a look at it."

Ryland said, "We might need Sykes to take a look at it in due course, if Nash needs the help, but we need a report implying it's badly damaged – so the thing can be listed as a write-off.

Nicholson knows what he's doing. Just get a situation report on the crash with a sort of a vague bottom line about the degree of damage. We'll just need it for the file. Then go and see Nicholson. I think he will fill you in."

"If you say so Sir."

Ron stopped off with Sykes to get the right forms reporting an "aircraft loss due to damage" before returning to the north hangar.

He found Nicholson poring over some maps. "We have submitted the reports on the Mosquito crash. Gather they will get it signed off without difficulty. Although I'm not clear what you intend for the aircraft – sorry – I should call it the 'wreckage' shouldn't I"

Nicholson grunted in acquiescence. "As you know by now, we operate in a somewhat shadowy world. The less equipment is traceable the more we like it. I've agreed with the CO of the experimental squadron that the aircraft will be written off. The flight was to check on the trim and balance because of unique new armament in her nose."

Ron had spotted the unusual feature of the mosquito. "You mean a somewhat large artillery piece someone had mounted at the front of the aeroplane?"

"You noticed it did you? It's a seven pound Molin's field cannon. De Havilland thought the mosquito could carry something heavy and were trying it out. It works. Fires at 30 rounds a minute with an auto loader. They were waiting to see if the War Department can use it. We think we may be able to, if no one else can."

Ron remarked "I see. So another ingredient in your impossible pie."

Nicholson picked up on the phrase. “Impossible pie? Certainly a tricky challenge I grant you. Is impossible your analysis? How do you weigh up the task?”

Ron did a bit of thinking out loud. “Let’s see. We have to learn about the target – know where he is – and reliably so. We have to get the message back here somehow. Then we need to arrange a pinpoint air raid – bearing in mind any bomber raid that gets within a mile of the target we think is accurate – and I mean literally a mile……”

“Go on.” prompted Nicholson.

“We then have to be sure the person bought it, the named person got killed I mean. We need to make sure he didn’t disappear down an air raid shelter or bunker or something.” Ron paused. “I would say it’s a tall order, but not impossible. Maybe we need to eat our impossible pie one bite at a time. I would suggest we list each area and try to come up with a solution for each bit.”

Nicholson began writing down some notes “Good plan. We’ve already got ideas about some of these. Is there anything else?”

Ron went on. “Secure communications – both for scouting and information gathering. But during Ops, well, I can imagine Jerry is intercepting our radio links.”

Nicholson paused in his note taking. “Of course we use code, so we hope it’s secure, but if agents get taken — or pilots for that matter….”

“I know a little bit about codes and I suppose you have been told that I have knowledge of the German language.” Ron assumed that someone knew about his background otherwise he might not have been here.

Nicholson nodded. “Indeed yes.”

Ron explained. “In fact the two – codes and German language – are linked. I did take an interest in encryption during my maths degree and anyway a lot of mathematical papers originated in Germany, so my German from school was needed. Watch your step about unbreakable codes, especially where our German friends are concerned.”

Ron thought it worth exploring another idea. “While we were talking about codes, let me try out something on you. Welsh.”

Nicholson looked puzzled. “Welsh? Who is Welsh?”

Ron Chuckled “Not who. Wales. Welsh. The ancient native Britons tongue, banished to the Celtic fringe.”

“Explain please.”

Ron did so. “Most coding, more or less, relies on substitution. Swap one letter or number for another using a set of rules known only to the sender and the person supposed to receive it. Anyone intercepting the message has to unscramble it. If the set of rules becomes known to others, the code is broken. The interceptor can read the message and other messages which use the same rules.”

Nicholson said, “That’s obvious, surely.”

“Yes, but to break the code you need as many clues as you can find. The most basic is the format you are expecting – which might be data like latitude and longitude, times, or other numeric data, but usually for messages there will be words in a language.”

Nicholson doodled with his pencil “So when we try to read messages from the enemy, we expect them to be in German and if they read ours, I suppose they’re looking for English.”

Ron picked up another pencil and began to write on a page in his notebook. "Yes, that's right." He turned the book round for Nicholson to read.

Ron had written *"Ydi'r llyfr ar y bwdd?"*

Nicholson tapped the pad with his finger. "Unreadable!"

Ron translated. "It says '*Is the book on the table?*' How many Germans would be able to twig to the full message, even if they had most of the letters? They would probably think the code was not working properly."

Nicholson saw the brilliance of the idea. "Excellent!"

Ron continued "You might also be able to risk a few voice transmissions, keeping it short. What I had in mind was calling in an air strike, but a bit risky I suppose. Anyway I have a Welsh speaker on my team, and wondered if this could be a start of trying something."

Nicholson had picked up the idea and was already formulating next steps "Yes, I think you're definitely onto something here. We obviously need a few more Welsh speakers than the single one you've got. I'll get on to the War Office and have a search organised by their personnel people. We'll be looking for Welsh speakers from any branch of the services. They'll have to have the right credentials before we get them involved, but surely there must be a few we can choose from."

Three days later Ron was sorting through invoices and statements in his office. He heard the door to the main office open and though the ribboned glass saw that all the staff in the outer office had stood up. Ron stood up too and moved to his door to see what was going on. He opened the door to see Group Captain Ryland. Ryland saw him in the doorway.

"So Cooper, this is where you hide when you're not over the North Hangar."

Ryland came in, amicably waving everyone else back to their posts. Ron pulled up a chair "Would you like a seat, Sir?"

Ryland shut the door and sat down. "Thanks. Sit down Cooper. You are to take a trip to London – you and Nicholson. And you're to bring your Welsh friend with you, what's his name?"

"Evans, Sir."

"You have important people to meet, Cooper – very important – needless to say I'm not completely in the picture, but it's Nicholson's show. He will brief you. Oh by the way, you might meet up with Joan Newcombe there. Apparently she's been doing some investigation on the personnel front for your North team."

Nicholson and Ron met up at the railway station. The usual route to and from Whittingsmore was by the local train that was the feeder to the main line between London and Nottingham. Trains were rarely busy, the passenger traffic consisting of civilians and military personnel in equal measure. Ron was travelling in uniform and as was the normal protocol for officers they had first class tickets. Nicholson was dressed as he usually was, in a grey flannel suit, overcoat and broad brimmed hat. They boarded the train, found an unoccupied compartment and sat opposite each other. With the sound of a whistle, the train jerked into motion.

Nicholson took his hat and coat off. "When we get to London, we will be doing two things today. Firstly, we need to interview six or seven candidates – they will be Welsh speakers and two or three of them might be foreign correspondents, if you catch my drift." He tapped the side of his nose. "Your Welsh speaker, where is he by the way?"

"Evans? He'll meet us there. He's had a bit of leave and some of the chaps said they would take him to London. Bit of an eye opener after rural Wales I reckon. There're under instruction to get him to the meeting though – and in good shape!"

It was a 'staff selection' day of sorts. Nicholson described what they intended. "We will be looking for candidates. Your Welsh speaker needs to try out the communication bit. Our lads will be looking for the other virtues they may or may not have. Two Paras and I think one in the Royal Marines and a mixture from other branches of the services. From our point of view, being able to use a parachute is probably a given. A WAAF officer called Joan Newcombe has been conducting a trawl through the personnel files."

Ron thought, "Well, well." He said drily "We've met actually."

Nicholson seemed unsurprised and indifferent. "Oh really? She is a very bright and capable officer. Anyway your man Evans will be given a sheet of questions and a telephone. The idea is, we test out communication by him ringing up the candidate, asking questions and seeing if we get clear communication over the phone. Of course the real thing will be over a crackling radio. Evans will need to translate the answer into English for it of course. Is his English up to that?"

"Oh yes I think so. Immersion in the RAF for four months has brought him on no end."

Nicholson carried on his explanation as the train rumbled and swayed over a set of points, the clatter momentarily breaking the increasing but regular rhythm of the wheels on the rails. "The second thing is we are meeting…." Nicholson stopped talking as a passenger passed the window of the compartment. Extra discretion, even though the door was closed. Nicholson resumed. "We are meeting an Assistant Director of secret intelligence. A chap called Dr James. They've got some news for us I gather – but I'm also hoping they'll have some wizardry to help us with accurate navigation. This chap James seems to have a direct line to Winston!"

They had to change trains after about half an hour, at Melton Mowbray. They stepped out of the train onto a platform wreathed in steam and watched as the coaches that had formed their train were drawn away. Nicholson said, "Better cut the chat about the job on the London train, it will be busier. Have you brought any reading matter?" Having something to do to fill time on train journeys was always a good idea – it was not too uncommon for some delays to last hours. A combination of air raids, unexploded bombs and disruption to overworked railway worker rosters could throw out the timetables.

"I've brought a couple of books, but I'm going to buy a paper." Ron pointed towards the kiosk on the platform next to where they were standing. The transaction completed, he returned and watched as the engine that had pulled their train, now detached from the coaches, trundled slowly back towards them and drew to a halt near where they stood. They felt the heat waft over them from the open firebox door which could be seen in the cab of the engine. The locomotive reversed onto another track, clearing the way for their London bound train that was already approaching the platform.

Ron had brought a Welsh language dictionary and a text book on encryption. He thought belatedly that anyone picking up his case might guess what they were up to. Feeling guilty over a theoretical and imagined breach of security, he wondered what Nicholson might be reading.

Ron asked him about his book. Nicholson replied. "How to Make Friends and Influence People" No-one would guess Nicholson's job from his reading matter! Ron laughed in a moment of black humour. Nicholson saw the irony and chuckled too. "Well it is a best seller, and I couldn't get a book called 'How to Find Enemies and Eliminate People', could I!

After arrival at St Pancras they walked through streets, passing various spots with bomb damage, but fewer than would indicate the total devastation that Ron expected. This part of London must have suffered less than others. They found a large anonymous-looking building where Rhys was waiting for them inside the entrance hall, none the worse for his experience of the capital. Ron decided not to ask about the Welshman's night on the town. After passing various security checks, Nicholson went one way and Ron and Rhys another, following directions given by the receptionist to navigate long corridors with many doors off. Ron found room 208, marked 'Personnel' with a small seating area outside. He said "Wait out here Rhys" and went in. He was directed to another door off the first room – he knocked and entered the office. As he stuck his head round the door he heard a familiar voice. "Hello Ron, fancy meeting you here!" Joan looked him up and down. "Your new uniform suits you."

When they had last met she outranked him somewhat. "Thank you, um – what am I supposed to call you now?"

Joan folded her arms and stood in a slightly provocatively way. "You, Ron, can call me Joan. But what should I call you?" Ron now had a higher rank and could afford the air of informality that was stifled before he had his commission. " 'Ron' will be fine, unless we are with the stuffy brass."

"We'll have to stay away from the stuffy brass then. Anyway, when do you to go back to base?"

Ron smiled. "Depends how we get on." The double meaning was deliberate. Ron was not sure what was planned or how long they would be in London. "What did you have in mind?"

They both knew they were flirting. "We better get on with the job. Have you got Evans with you?"

Ron nodded over his shoulder. "He's outside."

Joan assumed a transformation into a business-like demeanour. "Right. We've got six men to interview. They are on the other end of a telephone." She handed a sheet of paper to Ron. She waved casually over her shoulder towards the windows, all of which were adorned with taped crosses on each pane. "Evans rings up and asks them, in Welsh, to go to the window, look at the park opposite and say how many ducks there are on the pond, how far away it is and the number of trees round the pond. All in Welsh of course. He fills up this form here with the answers. It's supposed to be the sort of thing, distance, numbers and so on, that might need to be relayed in a secure way. The phone number he has to ring is on the top of the form.

Ron looked at the form. "Bayswater 2196?"

"That phone is actually in another wing of this place. For some reason I don't understand, that bit of the building is not on the internal telephone system. We're using the phone to check out voice communication. I gather the idea is that our Welsh speakers will be talking to one another over the radio – the telephone is supposed to simulate that. That's why we're not doing it face-to-face."

The telephone rang and Joan answered. She made a brief note and put the phone down. She passed the note to Ron. "You're wanted down the corridor. Here's the room number."

Ron picked up his stuff. "I'll wheel Evans in on my way out. See you later — I hope."

Ron bumped into Nicholson before he had gone a few strides down the maze of corridors. "Come on, we are going in the same direction" Nicholson said, leading the way.

Ron and Nicholson entered an oak panelled office with a long heavy oak conference table. There were two civilians already there, who stood politely as they entered. One knew Nicholson, it seemed. "Hello Nicholson. You must be Flight Lieutenant Cooper. This is Dr James. My name is Smith." They all shook hands. "Now, tell us how you are getting on with your plans." Smith was the older man of the two, probably in his forties, quite dapper with a handkerchief in his top breast pocket. James was younger, maybe under thirty and somehow gave a sort of thoughtful air, but this probably was Ron's imagination. Ron presumed from the title that James was a scientist of some sort with a PhD in goodness knows what.

They sat down and Nicholson launched into an explanation. "As you know we have the list and agents tracking a few of our target people, so that in broad terms we may be able to locate some of them. We've come up with a secure communication idea when we need to guide in a strike. There are things still to be solved of course, but the overall plan is this. The target person is located and we attack that location with a special Mosquito aircraft. It's got a seven pound Molin's field cannon with an automatic loader mounted in the nose. It packs quite a punch. We also have a Lancaster that flies a bit faster than normal – we know that speed helps us slip through – although not as quick as a Mosquito obviously, but we hope to follow up the Mosquito with a Lancaster and deposit a large bomb load on the target after that. Finally, and this depends on circumstances, but as soon as we can afterwards, we have a full scale bomber raid on the location."

Smith punctuated the story. "Sounds good if it all works."

Nicholson continued. "Yes, but there are some problems we hope you might be able to help us with. Accurate navigation. The job's too risky to attempt in full daylight and we don't stand a chance at night of finding the right spot. We plan to make our first mission on a target as close to home as we can to try everything out before venturing deep into enemy territory."

Smith turned to Dr James who had been sitting thoughtfully. "What do you think Dr James – you've not commented so far?"

"I was listening. First, let me respond to your navigation problem. There is a system called 'Oboe', but the RAF high command are not keen. We could set you up with that."

Ron followed the rule he had developed for himself of asking what he thought were reasonable questions, until told otherwise. In any case, it was not completely clear who was the senior man, although he guessed that was Smith. "I suppose I should ask why the RAF are not keen."

Dr James didn't mind answering. "Good question. It involves flying the attacking aircraft on a predictable route in the run up to the attack – actually it's a slightly curved route. They think it's very risky for a large bomber formation to follow such a predictable path on a regular basis. If the enemy found the route defined by the radio it would be a real problem. But I would think the way you're doing it with a single aircraft, followed up with another, might be okay."

Nicholson was decisive. "We'll take it."

James continued. "The Germans have various radio navigation beams you know. We keep finding the odd radar station for detecting incoming aircraft as well as generating these beams. The enemy would expect us to attack any we might find. Could your agents observe how effective the bombing accuracy using Oboe might be? I'm wondering if we can kill two birds with one stone."

Smith indulged in black humour. "Your metaphor is very interesting."

Nicholson checked his understating of the proposal. "You mean get someone to watch the attack and get them to tell us what happens in detail?"

James nodded. "Yes that's it."

Smith turned to Nicholson. "Now look, you've got the agents on the ground. Could you observe the attack and check out the accuracy of the radar navigation?"

Nicholson responded. "I'm not sure we haven't changed the subject, but we are not planning on attacking our targets by an automatic system. We just want to be sure we've got our man. To that extent we will be observing, but what we need to do is to get to the target precisely."

Dr James produced a map while he was talking. "Let's think about this. Your targets – the people – move about, and people do that. My German radar installations stay in the same place." Unfolding the map on the table he pointed to a location. "Here are the ones we know about. Could we combine any of your operations with an attack on a radar station, so the purpose is disguised?"

Nicholson took some documents out of his case. "Let's have a look." Checking a list, he pointed to the map. "Florrennes. What's that one?"

Dr James answered. "That's a radar transmitter used for radio defence – it's a type code-named Wurzburg. Do you have agents in that area?"

Nicholson looked at Smith. "Let's have a look at that." This was obviously serious stuff, a list of agents and their locations. Ron felt the hairs on the back of his neck prickle. Ron and Nicholson both produced a list and matched them up on the table. Generally kept seperate, this was an extra security measure in case of loss.

Nicholson scrutinised the matched lists, another document and the map. "Not only do we have agents, we have a very nasty individual on the list of target persons. He's called Bauer and he's set himself up in a Chateau near Saint Aubin. Where is your radar?"

There was a knock at the door and everyone, in an almost synchronised movement, turned their papers over or slid them back into their cases. Smith rose and went to the door and opened it to a lady with a tea trolley. With a series of deferential pleasantries, she poured out four cups and left the trolley and disappeared back out into the corridor. Smith made sure the door was closed. The cups were handed round and all the papers then reappeared. The map was unfolded again. Nicholson resumed "We were just checking where this radar station is."

James produced a slide rule. "Well let's have a look at that." Muttering to himself "Latitude 50, 16 east, longitude 4, 40 north …. um let's see.

Ron could see the grid lines and legend on the map. "It's got to be close."

Nicholson agreed. "Certainly they're only a few miles apart so we could navigate by using, what do you call it? Oboe? Then go for Herr Bauer at the same time."

Ron presumed Pythagoras calculations were the subject of the slide rule arithmetic, when James exclaimed . "Gosh! The Chateau and the radar station are only 1.1 miles apart."

Smith saw possibilities. "This looks like a good opportunity for two hits and a good cover story to me. Who is the target from the list?"

Nicholson replied. "As I say, the chap's called Bauer. What do we know about him…?" He looked at more papers. "Right. Mass murder of Jews, deportations. Capture and torture of resistance fighters. We seem to think he shot some Jewish children in front of their parents."

Ron was shocked even though he had come to expect stuff like this. "God! Nasty. I can suddenly see why we have a list!"

James stated the obvious. "The Nazis have some very unsavoury people – let's say you wouldn't want them in your club." Ron wondered obtusely what sort of club Dr James might be familiar with – he didn't look like the sort that frequented gentlemen's clubs or a rugby club – but decided he might be a golfer. James was still speaking, while Ron was musing on his pointless speculation. "How long to get ready for this raid, on Florrennes, I mean? Bearing in mind this is just the warm-up show for another important target I want to tell you about."

Nicholson implied a question in response. "Need to think about it – give us a month?"

Smith asserted his control of the meeting "You've got three weeks – if you can do it in less – okay. We need to make sure your tactics work. The job after this one absolutely must succeed and we want that one quick. But mostly we want to be sure of the hit. Dr James?"

"Four days ago the RAF intercepted a German photo reconnaissance aircraft over Warwickshire. They managed to force it down and capture the whole thing intact. These are the photographs that had been taken by the German recon camera." He gently tossed the photographs onto the table. They slid and fanned out across the varnished table top, almost like laying out a hand of cards. "The fighter boys are going to be mentioned in despatches – you'll see why in a minute."

Ron flicked through the photographs "These photographs all seem to be country houses of one sort or another."

James produced more stuff from his briefcase and put the contents on the table. "Exactly, there's more. This was with the pilot's papers. He pushed the papers across the varnished surface towards Ron." How's your German?"

Ron could see it was no time for false modesty. "Its okay. Let's have a look."

Dr James made a wave of his hand and smiled gently. "Actually I've got a translation here, but feel free."

Ron shuffled through the papers. They were clearly formalised and signed off military documents of various types – the RAF did not have the monopoly on forms and paperwork. "Well, there are orders authorised by a chap called Hartmann. It's a common name I think. We just have a name, no rank or initials. Actually this paper might be better described as a briefing document. What does your translation call it?"

James replied. "Says orders – but might be instructional information because of the content. It is telling the crew to search for country houses possibly with accommodation or ancillary buildings. Also anything with radio aerials."

Nicholson had been looking at his 'list' of important and some nasty people. "I've got a chap down here called Professor Hartmann."

Ron sat up straight. "I met a German Professor Hartmann in 1936 or 37 – could it be the same man?"

Nicholson studied his list a bit more. "Our man is a mathematics professor specialising in encryption."

"It is the same man! He came to the University when I was an undergraduate. There was a sort of exchange between the Universities. Two of their undergraduates and this Professor Hartmann. It was a seminar about number systems applied to encryption and codes. What a coincidence!"

"You being here is just to create the likelihood of that sort of coincidence. So, Hartmann – that fits." Smith too was flicking through papers. "We think he is leading a team involved in codes and code breaking. We had thought he was either trying to break codes or trying to find our Station X. We now know he is doing both."

Ron asked one of those questions that pushed the boundaries. "Should I know what Station X is?"

"Definitely not!" exclaimed Dr James. "Well, not up until now. I suppose this is the point when we should tell you." James looked round the room at the others, apparently seeking a degree of acquiescence in a silent exchange of looks. As a relative outsider, to SOE, Ron had noticed that the strict hierarchy he was used to in the RAF was much more blurred within this group of people. Apparently there was no negative body language from the others and James resumed, "Station X is a code breaking section we have set up. Like many other of our outstations we set it up in the country – it's based in a country house."

Ron could see the country houses in the pictures. It seemed for a moment that the enemy had found Station X. "Is that what the German reconnaissance aircraft has photographed?"

"No, they haven't found it – but it seems they are looking for the right sort of thing – well right from their point of view. The place they actually had on film is Ashorne Hill –that's where the strategic centre for iron and steel supply has been set up. The worry is, that if they keep looking, they'll find Station X. The team at Station X is absolutely vital to the war effort. You see we know quite a lot about the German code system."

Ron said, "I think they've got a coding machine."

James looked taken by surprise by this statement from Ron. "Oh really? What makes you say that?"

"The two graduates were quite friendly, bearing in mind this was 1938 I think, but the Prof was a really obnoxious bloke. Very arrogant. Just before the end of the seminar there was a bit of an incident."

Smith chipped in. "An incident?"

Ron twiddled a pencil "Yup. There were only about 12 of us there, but he, Hartmann, suddenly realised that we had a Jewish lad with us. Professor Hartmann never turned up to the final tutorials and left – in a huff we presumed. Before they went back to Germany, one of the German undergraduates told me that the Prof was an ardent Nazi and that Hartmann couldn't bear to be in the same room as the Jewish lad from our university. He confided in me that he himself was a quarter Jewish."

Smith commented. "Surprised he revealed that, given the situation – you know, with his Professor and all."

"We got on quite well – socialised quite a bit in the time that he was over. He was keen to keep on the right side of the Prof, as a government job depended upon it. We exchanged letters a bit – before the war started."

Smith asked, "What was his name – the student I mean?"

"Wolfgang Shultze."

Nicholson was digging through a sheaf of papers again. "I think we know that name too. Doesn't he show up on the Sweden manifest?" He soon found the name. "Yes, here we are. Yes, someone called Wolfgang Shultze has been to Sweden – to Gotenberg and Stockholm at least twice in the past seven months."

Ron was even more intrigued by these apparent coincidences. He reflected on the laws of probability. His new superiors could find all sorts of things out and knowing about the areas of academic work Ron had been associated with – and the people he had met – perhaps it was not too surprising. "Is it the same bloke? What is the Sweden manifest?"

Nicholson said "The Sweden manifest is a name we call a specific bit of intelligence. Merchant ships plying to Sweden from Germany obviously have a manifest of what and who is aboard. We happen to have a source at Gotenberg that sometimes can pass that information to us. Sweden is a place that provides some important war materials – to both sides – but Germany is much closer than Britain, so we try to keep a close eye on the traffic. Most of the crew or other personnel on these ships stay either on the ship or close to the port." Nicholson looked back at the file. "In the case of Herr Shultze he shows up as bit exceptional. When they land, foreign visitors have to tell the Swedes where they will be staying. If this report is to be believed, he travelled twice across Sweden to the German Embassy in Stockholm, stayed a few days than goes back. Now why would he do that?"

Smith said. "If it is your man from the University, codes will be the link. Perhaps he is a courier of some sort."

James turned back to Ron. "Maybe. You carry on with your story about why you think the Germans have a coding machine."

Ron continued recounting his university days. "Oh yes. We had gathered that they were working on a coding algorithm of some sort that could be automated. I can't remember much now, but we were discussing variable substitution codes."

Dr James gently tapped his pencil on the table thoughtfully. "This all fits. The Germans think they have an unbreakable code system. It is indeed based on a machine – we call it an Enigma. Nearly everyone in the German military and technical community agrees that it is unbreakable. For the German military to think it could be broken is considered as a sort of heresy. That said, the Navy were less than convinced about its absolute infallibility and have now beefed theirs up. The Naval machine has many more combinations, we don't quite know how many."

"If you know all this, I would guess that you have broken the – what do you call it – the Enigma code system."

Dr James looked at the others then back to Ron. "This is most secret." He paused. "We haven't quite broken Enigma, although from time to time we can read quite a proportion of their messages. We are desperate that they don't even get an inkling that we can penetrate their communications."

Smith pointed to Hartmann's name on the papers. "Prof Hartmann is the leading person advocating the theory that Enigma is not secure and that we have a well honed code-breaking team. One advantage for us, is that he is in the minority in German thinking. At the moment that is."

Nicholson chipped in. "I think I know why we're meeting today. I think this bloke is the one leading the search for codebreakers and is probably desperate to prove his colleagues incorrect – by showing we have such a team and then destroying it. That's why he's briefing the reconnaissance people to look for where Station X might be."

James nodded. "We won't say where Station X is, you don't need to know, but Harmann is not far off being on the right lines, having seen his briefing note and the photographs. At present it seems that Hartmann is out on a limb, politically I mean, but if he collects more evidence – it would be, well……"

Smith finished the sentence for him. "It would be better if he was accidentally killed in an RAF raid."

Chapter 7

After his long and revealing meeting with James, Smith and Nicholson, Ron had a lot to think about. At the other end of the building – in the Personnel Department – was Joan 'interviewing' some Welsh speakers with Rhys Evans. After a quick lunch and a few wrong turnings in the maze of corridors, Ron found his way back.

Joan was with Rhys. It looked like they were wrapping things up.

Ron asked "How did it go – have we established communication?"

Joan replied with a sort of giggle. "All okay apart from the wrong number!"

"What do you mean?"

Joan said, "Tell him Evans."

Evans was in on the joke it seemed. "We got about halfway through – but the next call a woman answered. I was expecting a bloke. I thought it better just to carry on. I'm still not sure how all this fits together."

Joan added, "I was listening in – goodness knows why, I wouldn't understand a word of it all those th, th, sounds."

Ron tutted, "Now, now."

Joan said, "She – the woman – she was very upmarket and said her husband was a local councillor and she didn't take kindly to nuisance calls. She seemed to know it was Welsh being spoken."

Evans explained more. "Thought I'd better cover up, so went into English and said sorry about the crossed line. I said I was checking up on a lost shipment of Welsh lamb. I pretended to be working from the Ministry of Supply. It was the first thing that came into my head."

Ron glanced at Joan and nodded. "Sounds like a good cover story on the spur of the moment."

Evans carried on. "Yes, but she seemed to panic a bit and we had a very funny conversation – and she was trying to find out more and more about me."

Joan was chuckling. "There's more. We thought we had better make sure about the security aspects and we managed to track the number and got onto the police through our Special Branch contacts. The first thing they did was ring the local Police station only to find out that moments before that, the lady in question had been onto to the sergeant there. She had rung the police to confess to handling lamb from the black market through her husband's butchery shops!"

Their laughter became infectious and maybe a release from the serious stuff going on all around them. Ron said "Crumbs. This is the second time I've been involved in meat scandals – maybe I should go into the meat trade after the war!"

After a few moments the three of them settled down and got back to business. Ron asked, "How did the rest go? The rest of the interviews I mean – the ones where you got the right number."

Rhys seemed pleased. "Yes. I was happy to talk to the boys, it was nice to hear Welsh spoken. Reminded me of home. No problem with the communication at all."

There was a knock at the door and Smith appeared. He nodded at Ron, and then said, "Joan, could I have a word?" He gestured for her to come with him.

"Sure." She rose and said to Ron and Rhys, "See you later" as she left with Smith.

Ron made a complete change of subject. "Evans, you told me you are pretty good with a shotgun."

"Yes of course. I was quite a good shot – rabbits mostly. I never missed."

"Ever been in an aeroplane – flying I mean?"

Evans wondered what the question could be about – surely his boss knew the answer. "No. Until I met you no one would even let me near anything."

Ron said "Good job that the recruiting boys didn't find out you're a good shot – they would have had you in the army. We find we do need you in the RAF."

"After all, it's nice to be wanted at last."

Ron came to the point. "It is quite specific. We want you to fire a big gun. It's a seven pounds artillery piece to be precise, but you will be pleased to know it's not for the army."

Evans knew straight away. "It's that special Mosquito, isn't it sir?"

Ron noticed momentarily that Evans' face flushed ever so slightly, then went a bit pale. Evans had worked it all out in a flash. Not surprising really from desk job and general dogsbody to the flying and some other stuff he did not yet know about.

"Yes it is the Mossie. And before you ask we don't want you to become a pilot. One of those men you just spoke to – not the lady! – will be telling you what to shoot at over the radio. It would be in Welsh of course. Do you reckon you can sit in the Mossie and guide the pilot to hit a target? You said you never miss."

Evans was seized with enthusiasm. "Well, not quite the same as a 12 bore shotgun shooting at a rabbit in the light of the torch, but sounds interesting."

"You'd get to practice with a crack pilot."

Evans said with a smirk, "As long as I don't have to talk to that lady again – now that was scary!"

They were just wrapping up when Smith and Nicholson came in.

Ron finished with his briefing to Evans. "We will get you teamed up with a pilot and some training. We can talk about it on the late train on the way back tonight."

Smith interjected with news for Ron. "I'm afraid your man here will be going back on his own." He turned to Evans. "We need your boss here."

This took Ron unawares. "Oh really? What's the story?" He saw that Evans had collected up his papers and Ron saw him out with a "Off you go Evans – looks like I've been set up with another job. See the Wing Co in the morning. He will know what to do to get you up in the air and shooting." He shut the door after the departing airman.

Smith said. "Brace yourself for a surprise or two."

Life was full of surprises on this job. Ron's reply was both quizzical and sceptical in tone despite its intended deference. "Oh yes?"

Smith pulled up a chair. "Sit down. Your friend Wolfgang Shultze works for Professor Hartmann. Not only that, we know where he is now. He is in a merchant ship sailing from Lübeck in northern Germany to Stockholm. The Sweden manifest is a list of passengers and goods that go between Germany and Sweden. Our agent works in the docks and finds out what and who is moving back and forth. Shultze is in Sweden – and not for the first time."

"Why would Wolfgang visit neutral Sweden?" Ron enquired.

"Our guess is that he is a messenger of some sort. We want you to meet him in Stockholm. We're flying the pair of you there tomorrow night. We have a high-speed passenger service courtesy of The British Overseas Airways Corporation.

There were a number of quickfire points for Ron to grasp – a trip abroad in wartime – by air – sounded a bit more adventurous than checking passes in the Orderly Room. Was he ready for that? Ron picked up on the first thought. "I didn't think there were any civilian flights."

Nicholson explained. "Actually they're the RAF, but it's a neutral country of course so things are not as they seem and you will be on diplomatic business."

Ron realised he had heard that a 'pair' of people were going. "Who is the other chap I'd be going with?"

Nicholson went on "We are very careful to avoid sending a man to neutral countries who is not on the regular embassy staff. A couple attract less interest. That's the theory anyway. I've just briefed Joan. She's going with you."

Ron blinked. "Wow! As you say, a bit of a surprise."

Smith assumed an ironic tone and raised his eybrows. "Unfortunately, I think it's important that you will have to tolerate a VIP lifestyle for the few days when you are there. Your normal every day Englishman is unlikely to be swanning around in Sweden. Your job is to meet Shulze and try and find out as much as you can. He knows you. Do you think you can hook up with him again?"

"I guess I have to. But what if he turns out to be difficult and doesn't want to co-operate?"

Smith had this covered. "You can offer him defection and protection – bringing him back to England. But the idea is to get him on our side, but still in place in his post. You will have to be absolutely sure about trust first before you give him any idea of our interest in codes and so on." Smith handed Ron a file tied up with black ribbon. "You said he was a quarter Jewish. This is the dirty bit. This is a file of documented atrocities against Jews. You might need to show him this to try and convince him to help us."

The following day was planned as a briefing for Ron and Joan. For some reason Ron could not imagine, the powers that be thought it best that much of the 'training' to go on a special mission to a neutral county was conducted with Joan and Ron in separate locations. This entailed being driven about between three different houses in north London, then back to the office they started from. There was a hell of a lot of waiting around between meetings with the four or five 'experts' including stuff on diplomatic niceties which Ron characterised as knowing with which implement to best disembowel one's Swedish fish course. They did however get measured for some smart civilian clothes to be picked up in Stockholm. A cover story didn't seem to exist, but then they weren't actually going to be on their own – the plan was to be with baby-sitters from the Embassy. Ron and Joan were just to look as if he was on some sort of floating attachment to the Embassy with his wife or fiancée. This seemed all very well and Ron was warming considerably to the plan. Until, that was, Ron was seen alone by a very serious and cold man who offered him a pistol and a suicide tablet. Ron instinctively refused both. But the man just shrugged and took them back. He wondered afterwards whether this was wise. As darkness fell, they were driven out of town to some aerodrome which was too dark to identify, even if Ron had any idea about this part of the country.

The first part of the trip was not really the VIP treatment as indicated by Smith. Far from it. The flight to Sweden was in a converted Mosquito bomb bay. The space was hardly designed for one, let alone two. A cot had been rigged up with two oxygen supplies and an intercom to the crew. There was a 30 minute briefing. Apparently the 'civilian' flights were not unusual although not quite routine. In case of enemy interception, the Mosquito could outrun most fighters if called upon to do so. So, there was an irregular service to and from neutral Sweden with diplomatic cargo, and it seems, occasional passengers. Ron got the distinct impression that two passengers at the same time was a bit of a first. This was confirmed when trying to get the pair of them into the space provided. After a struggle they managed to get in, with a few ribald remarks from the crew that squeezed them in. Ron would have expected nothing less.

They waited for take off, with some trepidation on Ron's part. They had been warned that conversation would be near impossible and to try to sleep. The MO had given them some pills.

Ron was very, very close to Joan even though they were both wrapped up in flying suits. "This is a turn up for the book. I hope I don't get air sick. I'm not very good in that department."

Joan was reassuring, but presumably was as jittery as Ron was. "The skipper says it will be a calm flight."

"Good job. Apart from the eyesight…" Ron removed his specs and clutched a sick bag, "I get travel sick sometimes. Some problem with my ears. I should think that's why I sit behind a desk rather than doing any more exciting job."

Joan seemed to be enjoying it. "This has turned out to be exciting hasn't it? Mind you this is a squeeze – it seems they've never had two passengers in this spot before."

Ron was slightly infected by Joan's positive attitude. "A squeeze yes, but I think of it as holiday with a lovely escort, paid for by the King, to a country not at war. Hum, yes it is a bit of a gift and exciting too. Let's hope we can justify it and look like a couple."

Joan response "I'm sure we can!" was drowned out by the sound of the first Merlin engine starting….

Chapter 8

A trip to another country would have been an eye-opener at any time for Ron. For Joan too, he guessed. However in the midst of the shortage and restrictions in Britain, Sweden was something else. For a start there was no blackout. Ron had forgotten what it felt like to move about at night and see where you were going. The promised VIP treatment had indeed materialised once out of the cramped belly of the Mosquito, although Ron had dozed through the flight and Joan seemed none the worse for it. They had disembarked – or rather fallen out of the bottom of the aeroplane – in a quiet hangar away from prying eyes. There they were met by Mr Perks from the embassy, who made it clear they could have anything they wanted. The embassy itself was like a five star hotel. By some feat of organisation, Ron and Joan had been fitted up with a suitable range of clothes. In Joan's case, the outfits made her look absolutely stunning in Ron's view. This was particularly so when they went out for the evening to try to meet up with their quarry.

Under the guidance of Perks from the embassy, they found themselves in a smart Stockholm restaurant. Joan had some fantastic outfit which was fairly revealing. If this was the embassy's idea of keeping a low profile, Ron wondered what making an impression would be like.

They took a table by the window and could see lights in the port twinkling through partially drawn curtains. No shout of 'put that light out' here. They talked over a meal which also exceeded the expectation of RAF-catered appetites.

Perks gave them a run-down on the situation over the meal. "We have observed Herr Schultze here on his two previous visits that we know about. He may have been to Stockholm any number of times, but if so, we didn't identify him then. This restaurant – it's one of the smartest in town. Like most young men, we suspect Schultze likes pretty girls, and the upmarket really attractive ones are found here – oh sorry miss."

Joan tossed her hair. "Don't worry about me – I know a little about male motivations."

Ron asked, "So what happens if he doesn't show up? I suppose there are other restaurants and bars."

"We will have to think again I suppose. We have an informant on the staff here who tells us about comings and goings. Assuming our information is correct, his routine was to come here for his evening meals, so we can expect him any time now. We do know he has checked in at the German embassy – it's about a 15 minute walk from here – we keep it under surveillance you see. That was a couple of hours ago. Allow time for freshening up and he would be due in the next hour. The Germans seem to give him a completely free rein."

Perks carried on. "We suggest Miss Newcombe approaches him first and starts a conversation. We can then get round to letting him know that Mr Cooper is here as well. We don't want him to panic and be scared off."

They dined well and even if it was a no-show, there were worse assignments. Perks nodded silently as a man of Ron's age entered. He hung his hat on a coat stand and moved to the bar. They all tried not to look and yet observe discretely.

Perks said nonchalantly, "I think that's him – he has gone to the bar. Is that him Mr Cooper?"

Ron didn't want to rush it. Having come all this way, it would look a bit silly to get the wrong person. "I can't quite see from here." He shuffled about in his seat waiting for the figure to face more towards him. "Hang on. It's some time since I've seen him you know." The room did not provide a clear and open view – there were screens, pot plants and other customers between them and the bar. Ron had been worried that recognition might not be certain, but when Schultze's face did come into view, his memory was clear and without doubt. "Yes, it is him, yes. What now?"

Joan said. "I think it's my turn now – isn't it?"

Perks went over it again. "So, Miss Newcombe will join him at the bar and strike up a conversation. Do you think you can manage that Miss?

Ron wondered if Perks was being a bit patronising – Joan was a cool operator.

Joan said light-heartedly, "I think so. He's quite good looking – you didn't tell me that Ron. Here goes."

Joan was indeed a natural – she seemed to be relishing the experience. She got up and Ron focused on her receding backside. She looked great. He mentally corrected himself – better keep his mind on the job. He watched her walk to the powder room, instead of going straight up to Schultze. For a long moment Ron thought Joan had lost the plot. "Where's she going?"

Perks had worked it out. "She is making it look perfectly normal, casual, rather than just going straight up to the bar."

Ron was concerned that in the gap Schultze would make off. Logic told him this was irrational anxiety, but then he was new to clandestine diplomacy. He said to Perks, in a whisper, "Do you do a lot of this?"

"Quite a bit, but there's no need to whisper. I should just try to act normally."

"I'll do my best in the situation, but it's not normal. It isn't for me anyway."

Joan soon returned from the direction of the cloakrooms, perched herself on a bar stool and quickly struck up a three-way conversation with Schultze and the barman. Ron felt very awkward, wanting to watch, but trying not to look. Ten minutes went by. The conversation looked like it was going well. Schultze took a break from paying close attention to Joan, and cast a glance around the room. Perks and Ron hoped that was the point where Ron's name had been introduced to the conversation, rather than Schultze becoming defensive and suspicious.

Joan made a subtle waving signal with her handbag.

Perks spotted it. "I think that's your signal to go to the cloakroom."

Ron didn't need telling twice – he was like a greyhound in a trap. Perks sensed his tension. "Don't rush."

"Ok. On my way." Ron made his best attempt at a casual walk to the cloakrooms without looking towards the bar. The plan was to first meet Schultze in the cloakroom rather than in the open area of the bar. There was an unstaffed desk and rows of coat hooks, mostly empty with a few coats and hats spread around. Ron checked between the rows of hooks. No one was around. Perhaps as well because they didn't have a plan if anyone else was there. Ron sat down to wait on a bench. No sooner had he done so, than Schultze appeared in the doorway.

Schultze seemed pleased to see Ron. Having been prepared by Joan a few minutes earlier, possibly the surprise was lessened a bit. Schultze greeted Ron in German. "It is you. How.... what are you doing here?"

Ron slipped easily back into conversation in Schultze's mother tongue. "Good to see you. We have a lot to catch up on. But this is not a good place to talk. Our countries are on different sides now and we must be discreet. Can we meet somewhere to talk?"

Schultze did not seem to have a problem with the suggestion. "Oh, yes. A small restaurant and coffee shop called Strom. It's in a street called Linnegaten between here and the central square – the Karlaplan. I find it very friendly. I come here when I want company and go there when I want to be quiet."

"It's seven thirty now – shall we say nine. Can you come alone?"

Schultze seemed content with the arrangements, receptive almost. "Yes, of course. Will you find it all right?"

Ron repeated the location. "The street is called Linnegaten and the cafe is called Strom. I think I'll find it." They left the cloakroom after their very short chat. Schultze went back to the bar and Ron to the toilets – something he found he needed with the tension of the last couple of hours.

Ron returned to the table where Perks and Joan were drinking coffee. Ron explained the conversation and the place for the next meeting. Perks said, "I know the place. I'll show you where it is and check the coast is clear."

Joan was interested in coming along. They discussed it and decided it would be best if Ron was alone. As they rose to leave, Ron picked up Joan's clutch handbag to pass it to her. It was somewhat heavy and unbalanced. "What do women put in handbags?" he said as he passed it to her. "Yours is very heavy."

"Thanks" she said as she took it. "In my case it's an automatic pistol. Don't you have one?" Ron was dumbstruck.

They went back to the Embassy accommodation together. Ron saw Joan to her room, while Perks went off to set up some discreet surveillance for Ron's meeting in the next hour. Joan invited Ron in and he asked about the gun. Joan seemed to think carrying a gun in her handbag was perfectly normal. Ron said, "I was offered a gun, but I instinctively turned it down because I didn't think I could use one. Never crossed my mind I might need one."

Joan said, "Well, I think you should have one tonight – take mine."

Ron realised he had been a bit naïve. Schultze had agreed to the meeting quickly. Could it be trap? He cannot have known he was going to be approached, but had a ready rendezvous suggestion. Was it gong to be safe? Perks was going to be watching out for him – with others – but at the key point Ron would be on his own. He would take the gun.

Joan handed over the pistol then kissed him. "Be careful". An initial peck on the lips, somehow turned into a full-on, prolonged passionate kiss. This further churned up Ron's mixed emotions, but he wasn't complaining. "Come straight back here and let me know how you get on. Doesn't matter how late – I'll be here."

Perks guided Ron to the café. Ron said, "I thought you fixed up for us to be watched – there's no-one else around."

"There is," responded Perks. "If you could see them they wouldn't be much good would they?"

Ron was slightly reassured that the eyes that could not be seen were watching. They stepped into a shadow and waited opposite the café Strom. At five to nine, they saw Schultze arrive. He was alone and looked unsuspicious and entered the café without hesitation. Ron had the package with the evidence of atrocities against Jews in his hand and felt the weight of the pistol in his pocket. He strode into the café leaving Perks on watch outside.

Schultze still had his coat on and turned to see Ron. His face lit up. Speaking in German he said, "Good evening again." He took Ron by the hand and shook it enthusiastically. "Come on, there is a back room. I have met a couple of girls in the restaurant where I met you – and have come here with them afterwards – to talk you understand."
Ron said, "I see."

"The lady I met tonight, is she your girlfriend? She is very nice."

Ron wanted to say 'yes' after that kiss. "In a manner of speaking, yes." Ron took a chair and they sat down, ordering a coffee. When the waiter had gone Schultze resumed – he was doing all the talking. They talked about their meeting at University those years ago and about common acquaintances – but it was hopeless trying to work out what had happened to them since then or where they might be, with the whole of Europe in turmoil.

Schultze said, "I have been here a few times before. I try to make the best of it. It's pleasant here in a neutral country and frankly Germany is quite depressing."

Ron responded, "We are on different sides now, not just a couple of carefree students as we were when we met in 1938."

"This is sad, but I'm not sure whose side I am on."

Ron said, "I think I know what you mean. I've heard what's going on in Nazi Germany – and you are part Jewish aren't you?

Schultze looked horrified. "Did I tell you that? I must have been mad!"

Ron observed, "You'd had a couple of beers."

"What is happening in Germany you can't guess. Some of my family have disappeared – a couple of Jewish cousins and an uncle."

Ron corrected him. "I can guess. We know the Nazis are persecuting Jews. We also know about the deportation and the murders."

Schultze was questioning. "How do you know this? I have feared that Jews may be being murdered, but you know…. Where do you fit in Ron?

"I am in the Royal Air Force."

Schultze looked impressed. "Flying Spitfires?"

Ron waved his hand. "No, no. Just administration."

"How is it you are in Sweden?"

"I came to see you."

Schultze sat up straight. "You knew I was here?"

Ron went for broke. "Yes, I think you have a government job with Professor Hartmann."

"You seem to know a lot, but you are right, I am working for Hartmann. That man is a real swine. What else do you know?"

"I think you are working with codes."

Schultze said, "I see. I am thinking you are going to ask me to help you. Look Ron, I am German but I have no love for the Nazis. I really don't know what to do."

Ron had brought the file not knowing if it would be of use or not. He decided to show it to Schultze. "Do you know how bad it is – for the Jews and the others, I mean? Do you know what the free world is fighting?" He took the file out of a large envelope and pushed the stuff across the table.

Schultze started sifting through the contents. "I have my suspicions, but how bad can it be?"

"I brought this file so you could see the evidence, the proof. It is shocking as you can see."

Schultze spent a few minutes looking through the file before pushing it away in shock and horror. Bad enough for any sane person; if you had friends and relatives who might be on the receiving end of vile treatment, it would be traumatic.

Ron wondered if he had done the wrong thing. "I am sorry I had to show it to you. I'm sorry I saw it myself."

Schultze took out a handkerchief and wiped his eyes, took a sip of coffee. "What should I do Ron?"

"You should do what you think is right, Wolfgang."

There was a long silence. Schultze was moved and upset. "After today nothing will be the same."

"You could come back to England with me and help locate Hartmann and his operation. This is one option."

With a resigned sigh, Schultze made his decision. "I will help you, but I can't leave, I am sure my family would suffer. Tell me what you want."

Perks saw Ron emerge from the cafe after about an hour and start to walk back towards the embassy. Discreetly following Ron's footsteps, Perks caught him up and then escorted him back to the embassy accommodation. Perks reported that the watch on the café had not picked up any unusual activity in the cafe or the street outside.

They walked through quiet streets and slipped back into the British Embassy. Ron returned to his room, took the file of Nazi atrocities and locked it in a drawer. The room was quite plush and had its own bathroom, with a shower. Showers were quite unusual in England and Ron remembered he had been in a cold sweat of anxiety while waiting for his role in the meetings with Wolfgang Schultze. He undressed and showered.

As the water stung his skin he reflected on the evening's events, most recently the meeting in the café. He guessed the meeting had gone as well as could have been expected, although maybe more by good fortune than good planning. Despite his late realisation, after Joan's promptings, that the selected meeting place might be a trap, Ron had then forgotten this risk as soon as he had walked into the café. He now thought himself a very amateur secret agent – he had not been cautious either in the café or in the room at the back, blithely accepting the invitation to meet with Schultze alone. He had got away with it, trusting that the conversations with Schultze had been open and genuine. Assuming this was the case, the meeting had been successful. Even if the exchange had been somewhat emotional, a commitment to cooperation had been readily forthcoming. Ron had also formulated a plan which would carry the whole job forward and would also be a test to see if Wolfgang Schultze was genuinely on board.

He dried himself and returned to the bedroom. Joan's pistol was lying on the bed where he had put it before showering. He looked at his watch. It was only ten twenty. Joan had said she wanted to see him on his return. He needed to give the pistol back and to brief someone else on his plan. More than that, Ron wanted to see Joan. He remembered the farewell kiss. Also – another sign of his self-assessed amateurism –he wanted to tell someone about the meeting. Perks had no interest in, or knowledge of, the mission Joan and Ron were on – he was just looking after their security and support in Sweden. He pulled on a pair of trousers and a shirt. He crossed the corridor and knocked at Joan's door. Clearly, she had been waiting for his return, opening the door immediately. Dressed in a silken figure-hugging nightgown, she embraced Ron as soon as the door was closed. She recoiled, as she felt the cold mass of the pistol stuck in his waistband.

"Ah", he said, withdrawing it gingerly by the handle. She took it from him, "Let's put this over here shall we?" She turned and placed the pistol on a table. The gown exposed a good part of Joan's back and clung to her buttocks. Ron reached out and stroked down her spine and let his fingers smooth over her bottom. She embraced him again and whispered in his ear, "Glad to see you back in one piece and in good form." As she spoke her hand slipped inside his open shirt front where the top few buttons had been left undone, her hand cool on his skin.

Their lovemaking was hugely satisfying, releasing pent-up feeling that had been bubbling for days culminating in the shared tensions of the meetings and the mission. After the sex it was easier to talk. Pillow talk.

Joan asked, "How did it go?"

"Great, fantastic, out of this world"

She elbowed him. "Not that – the meeting!"

"Oh yes that – sorry – yes. Wolfgang you mean."

He swung his legs round to sit on the edge of the bed. He took a drink of water from a glass on the bedside table. "It was painful. He's having a fraught time. His family have been victimised. He says he will help us and he is genuine I'm sure." Joan was at least partly in on the main plot, unlike Perks, and he needed to make sure someone else knew about the progress.

"I think Wolfgang will co-operate to the maximum. He is in a position to send us information. I suppose I shouldn't tell you everything Joan, its better you don't know the full details, but I've set up another meeting with Wolfgang before he goes back to Germany – he is giving us a leaving present."

"A present?"

"One of his jobs is to bring new code books to Sweden – for the Embassy – and take the old expired ones back. They change them regularly, but the validity overlaps by two to three weeks to cover any delays. He is going to drop off the old codebook with us, discreetly I hope."

Joan saw a flaw in the plan. "Surely they will want their code book back. If he turns up without it, there's bound to be lots of questions. Just saying it's been misplaced is hardly going to go down well."

"Quite. His return trip involves a train ride to Gothenberg and then a trip by ship back to Germany. My thought was that the ship offers an opportunity to 'lose' the codebook. He needs to find an excuse to throw the secrets bag over the side of the ship. He tells me the codebook print washes off in seawater immediately. This is how the

German Navy keep their code books secure. He will stuff the bag with a local newspaper and chuck it over the side in full view of someone. We need to give him an excuse to throw it away."

"How will you give him an excuse? I don't understand."

"I will send a message to London tomorrow. We ask London for a feigned attack on the Sonnenblick – the German merchant ship he is travelling on. We know when it's leaving and its destination. I just hope they can do it."

Joan understood now. "So as soon as it looks like an attack, Wolfgang chucks the bag away and the copy he leaves with us will not be missed."

"Exactly."

*

Ron and Joan spent a further two days in Stockholm, enjoying the sights and one another. A flight home was organised, utilising the same transport method by which they had come to Sweden. Two further meetings with Schultze were arranged, which Ron worried might be pushing their luck by risking discovery. Ron took Joan along to the next rendezvous, as they thought this was less likely to attract attention than repeating meetings with Ron and Wolfgang one to one. Wolfgang was charming to Joan, who appreciated his courtesy.

The day before their flight, Ron had a final meeting to pick up the expiring code books. The old friends bade one another a fond farewell, knowing that they might never meet again. Back at the embassy, Ron looked through the books, but not being too sure what to expect, could not be absolutely sure they were the real thing. It would have to be checked out back in Britain – they needed to get back with all speed.

Chapter 9

As soon as they landed, Ron called Nicholson on a scrambler telephone. It was just after dawn and it took some time to find Nicholson, but he sounded alert despite the early hour. Ron, though, did not feel great. The flight home in the belly of the fighter bomber was not as good as the outward trip, despite the close proximity of Joan. Joan seemed quite ok and disappeared off to freshen up somewhere. Ron would have liked to flop into a bed somewhere, but wanted to give as much notice as he could to RAF Ops, so they could stage a dummy attack on the German merchantman that was taking Schultze back to Germany. He had no idea how essential or effective this idea would be, but he wanted to maximise the chances of Schultze not being compromised. If the loss of the codebooks was fully disguised it would be a huge boost to the chances of success and protection for Schultze.

Ron had sent some messages from the Embassy in Stockholm, but knew only too well that codes were never unbreakable. He had been careful about the information he had sent. Now they were back in Blighty, it was worth clarifying the ruse.

Nicholson got straight onto Ryland, who agreed that he would try to get an air attack diverted to the waters off Sweden. All they had to do was strafe the ship – if they could find it.

Ryland called Askew into his office. Simon Askew looked haggard. He had been on Ops that night and only had 3 hours sleep. Ryland thought he should have been kinder on his Squadron Leader, but then he needed his advice. Askew pointed out the practical difficulties for our Bomber Command group. "It's not really our thing sir, but I tell you who might like it. The Canadians over at 418 Squadron – they are an intruder operation. They maraud about attacking anything that takes their fancy. Shooting up a ship in the Kattegat sounds like them. How long have we got to fix it up?

"The ship leaves Gothenburg at 0630 tomorrow, on the tide, bound for Lubeck."

"Ok sir, we know the time and the route, so finding the target is not completely hopeless as long as 418 have the weather on their side."

"Thanks Simon, sorry to get you over here after a hard night, but I needed your input. I'll get onto the Canadians."

*

Ryland rose early the next day and drove over to air operations command HQ. There was a huge plotting table with a map which was supposed to show all the air activity in northern Europe. WAAFS were pushing models about on the map. Almost as soon as he got there, there was bad news. The officer in charge approached him straight way. "Sorry sir, 418 Squadron's operation has been scrubbed."

Ryland was not amused. "Why, in God's name and when?"

"Both aircraft had problems and had to turn back."

"Both of them?" Ryland had lost his characteristic calm and was making the more junior officer uncomfortable.

"Were not sure why Sir. One had engine trouble after about an hour and the other has just lost contact after a mayday – this was five minutes ago."

The Canadian 418 squadron had relatively elderly Boston aircraft, although they were due to be equipped with Mosquitoes soon. A number of senior officers knew that the Bostons did not have a good success record.

Ryland looked at his watch. The ship was sailing in half and hour and Gothenburg was a long way. He looked down at the plotting table from the viewing gallery which was set high up on the wall to give the senior officers an overview of the situation. All the action seemed to be friendly aircraft coming home, nearing England. There was almost nothing in the North Sea except some models of ships, not aircraft. There was also a red cube with a swastika on it in Gothenburg. Their target – the Sonnenblick.

Ryland pointed at the group of ships some way off the Norwegian coast. "What's that?

"Naval destroyer task group, on anti-submarine work sir. We show it to keep our flyers out of trouble."

"And this?" Ryland pointed to another block that seemed to represent neither ship nor aircraft.

The officer looked the code number up on a pad. "Coastal Command flying boat sir, on attachment to the naval task force looking for subs."

*

The big Sunderland flying boat droned over the grey featureless waters of the North Sea. From the flight deck they could just make out smoke from the task force they were supporting, steaming to the North West. The crew looked out in all directions. The chance of spotting a periscope was not great, but if and when they found a U- boat they would be on it quicker than a destroyer and the Sunderland could pack a punch.

The radio operator appeared and handed a message to the co-pilot.

He read it and shouted to the pilot. “Message from Ops. Says to divert immediately to attack a German merchant ship in the Kattegat.”

The pilot responded “We’ve only got depth charges. How can we mount an effective attack on a surface ship?”

The co-pilot gave a further digest of the message. “There is a description of the ship, the Sonnenblick – two funnels, single fore mast leaving Gothenburg and heading for Lubeck. It says to harass it but do not destroy.”

“Attack but do not destroy, what does that mean? Ok. Plot us a course. And set the depth charges to minimum depth – we will do our best to damage her.”

*

The Captain of the Sonnenblick said goodbye to the Swedish pilot and watched the pilot’s tender edge away from the ship and back to Gothenburg harbour. The smaller vessel bobbed and corkscrewed away through the swell created by the wake of the Sonnenblick as the captain headed straight out to sea. The Sonnenblick was on a course which put the coast directly behind the stern, as requested by the harbour authority. The Swedes were happy to trade with the belligerents but liked to minimise the number of vessels from the Axis and the Allies that might be in their territorial waters. Not that there would be many Allied vessels in Swedish waters, after all they were surrounded by German occupied territories. Keeping neutral was a tricky business.

Having seen the ship out to sea, the Captain walked round the ship, casting an eye over the hold, and then went back to his cabin. He completed the log and looked through the manifest. Mostly engineering materials, as on previous runs. The crates of ball bearings he was supposed to collect were fewer than ordered. The port agent seemed to think they were in short supply. There were stainless steel sections, other manufacturing material and components, plus some food stuffs. And of course Schultze.

Schultze had travelled with the ship several times before. The Captain knew he was on some kind of government business, but knew better than to enquire what it might be. He didn't stay around the port but he was always back on time for the departure. No doubt he had been chosen for the job, whatever that was, for his reliability. On board he mostly kept himself to himself – he did a lot of reading and making notes. Occasionally he played chess with any of the crew that had the time – and Schultze was good at chess. No one had come near beating him. The Captain went back to the bridge by way of Schultze's cabin. The authorities wanted him looked after in a low-key way and as Captain, his job was to do that. This run around the Baltic and the Kattegat suited the Captain well and he wanted to keep it like that. There were far worse jobs – even though the crew might be a bit long in the tooth. All the young men had been whisked off to the Kriegsmarine.

Schultze was in his cabin reading. The Captain knocked on the open hatch as he passed. "Game of chess later?"

Schultze waved in assent as the Captain left and went back to the bridge. He nodded to the first officer on the bridge and scanned around. They were well out in the open sea, although they could just make out land on the horizon. No other vessels were in sight. They were heading south. A steward came up the steps with coffee and left the mug on a ledge for the skipper. On the way out he stopped outside the doorway, looking back down towards the stern of the ship. "Captain!" He pointed back toward the aft quarter.

The Captain crossed to the door and looked back. An aircraft was heading their way, not quite dead astern. As it approached it grew large – very large. It flew straight over the ship, so close that they could see the crew looking at them. They could also see the British markings.

The Captain hit a lever and a klaxon sounded. "Avoiding action!" he shouted and the helmsman spun the wheel over. They had small arms and a mounted gun of sorts, but it had never been fired. The crew's military preparedness had never been tested – they had never needed it before. The big flying boat was coming round gaining height. The first deck hand to pick up a machine gun started firing in the general direction of the aircraft. It looked like panic stations rather than action stations.

The Captain looked towards their gun emplacement where two crewmen were struggling to remove a tarpaulin. He also noticed in the melee that Schultze had emerged from below from a hatch next to the gun emplacement. The gun crew were too slow with the weapons and the flying boat was firing from its forward turret and splashes danced in the sea towards the ship. Schultze fell as he ran and the ship lurched. Two huge explosions made water spouts each side of the ship as the aircraft passed overhead with more gunfire coming from the rear turret as it turned for a second pass.

At last, the ship's only mounted gun started firing to join the cacophony of small arms fire that was directed at the attacker. None of it was having much effect as the flying boat had gained height and dropped a string of cylinders into the sea around their vessel. They kept firing, but there were further explosions in the sea which rocked the ship and drenched it from bow to stern. But there were no direct hits. The main gun had stopped firing. The captain saw that the crewmen had been knocked over by the water splashes. Schultze was next to them. Schultze rose from the deck and threw a package of some sort towards the sea, but the gusting wind was coming from that quarter and it blew back and fell to the lower deck. Schultze went to the railing. Both he and the Captain could see the bag sloshing around on the wet deck.

The flying boat was evidently breaking off the attack – it just kept flying north away for the ship. The Captain gratefully watched its size recede. Either they had run out of munitions or they had driven it off. Though he wanted to believe it, he knew the latter was not a likely explanation.

The helmsman steadied the ship and the Captain collected his thoughts. What had Schultze being doing? He saw that he was on his way to the lower deck, no doubt to pick up the sodden package.

The Captain went to the door pointed at Schultze and shouted to the gun crew. "Stop him and bring him here – and that package."

Schultze was grabbed and forced up the steps and onto the bridge. The captain wanted to make sure that the immediate danger had passed, before dealing with Schultze. "Check that the British plane has gone."

The bridge officer produced binoculars. "Yes captain, it's nearly out of sight to the north."

"Send a signal to Lubeck telling them about the attack and make full speed. We don't want to be caught again. And let's have a damage report"

He turned to the deck hand who had brought Schultze to the bridge. "What do we have here?

"He was trying to throw this over the side, Captain." He held out a leather satchel. The captain took it, finding it rather heavy for its size, even allowing for it being full of water.

"I can see that you are not a seaman my friend – you must allow for the wind. It's no good throwing things over on the windward side – the draft will throw them back onto the deck." So far, it seems the only damage to the ship from the British attack is your bag – it's soaking wet. So, what were you up to?"

Schultze did not respond "Nothing to say? Well let's have a look in your bag."

The Captain undid the buckle and lifted the flap of the bag.

Schultze took a quick backward step and pulled out a luger pistol from his soaking pocket. "Unfortunately Captain, I can't let you do that. Stop right there." He was calm, but with a gun in his hand, authoritative. He backed away so all the crew on the bridge were in his potential zone of fire. "Captain, you can show me how to throw a bag overboard properly." He gesticulated toward the door. "Move!"

The captain had little choice. Schultze shepparded the crew out onto the walkway. "Throw it! Now!"

With an unexpected athleticism the Captain hurled the heavy bag into the air, where the breeze caught it and carried into the sea, some distance from the ship.

The Captain and crew stood still awaiting the next instruction. Schultze said "Let us go back inside." Once back on the bridge he said, "Thank you Captain. I, Wolfgang Schultze travel in the service of the Reich. Now the bag is gone I need bother you no further, so please take my weapon." He turned the pistol in his hand and presented it to the Captain.

The Captain did not need telling twice. "My God!" He snatched the luger and instructed the crew. "Take this man and confine him to a cabin until we get to port. We will see then."

They kept Schultze in his cabin until they were tied up alongside the quay at the port of Lubeck. As the gangway was extended, the first person aboard was a uniformed SS officer who was met by the Captain. He was very smart in contrast to the dress of the scruffy team on his ship. He looked every inch the blond blue-eyed Aryan hero portrayed in the propaganda films. He gave a Nazi salute, "Heil Hitler!" and the Captain made a perfunctory and sloppy traditional salute in reply,then ordered Schultze to be brought up from his cabin. While they waited the Captain felt uncomfortable. Smartly turned out in impeccable military style he may have been, but the SS man had a sinister air about him.

Schultze was brought out but was restrained by two of the Sonnenblick crew, one on each arm.

"So Captain, this man threw his bag overboard when the British attacked?"

"Yes. We managed to recover the bag when the wind blew it back onto the deck."

"Did you see what was in it?"

"We took it from him – it was sodden. The deck was flooded you see, but this man pulled his gun when I looked inside and then he made me throw it overboard." With a perverted show of pride that he immediately thought unwise the Captain said, "I was more successful than he was."

"So it ended up in the sea." The Officer repeated the question. "But you did not see the contents of the bag?"

"No, well yes, it was just a bunch of wet paper. There were blocks of metal in it – lead weights I would guess. It was heavy."

The Officer's face brightened up from the interrogative demeanour he had previously shown. "Good, well done. Captain, you were not to know that Herr Schultze here has instructions to do exactly as he did if there was a risk of capture. Please, let him go." He turned to Schultze, "If there is a next time, Schultze, try to get it into the sea." He smiled and clapped them both on the back. "Perhaps Captain, you could return his weapon."

*

Joan and Ron returned to London where they met up with Smith and Nicholson.

Nicholson said, "From your signals, it looks like you had a successful trip."

Joan said "What about Wolfgang… Schultze I mean?"

Nicholson said, "Our contact at the port tells us he boarded the Sonnenblick. I guess you mean about the cover story – the dummy attack on the ship. We had a bit of trouble with an attack, but managed to improvise. Coastal Command sent a Sunderland flying boat that was in the area. The daft buggers tried to sink the ship but luckily they failed."

Smith said, "So the ruse has the best chance of working, but we can't be sure. Come on then, what was it that you got from Schultze?

Ron opened an attache case and put the code books on the table. "These. They are expiring code books for the last three months, but they still have current pages for the next 17 days."

Smith was impressed. “This is good, very good. We must get them to Station X straight away.” He made a phone call. “Yes, yes, we need some train times please.....yes to Leicester, I think.” Ron caught Joan’s eye as they waited for the call to finish. Ron wondered what she was thinking.

Smith had finished the call. “You two will take a train back to Leicester, and on to Whittingsmore, but we will get a courier from Station X to meet you on the train to take the code books from you.”

There was a knock at the door and a secretary entered with train times. “Here you are sir. There’s a train to Leicester at 1530 hrs.

Smith looked at the list. “Oh yes, that’s one of our regular runs. The courier will meet you at Bedford. You will be accompanied by a member of our team, technically a King’s Messenger. He’s worked the run before. Joan, can you fix it all up with personnel here, and tell them at Whittingsmoor that you are coming back today?”

“Sure,” she said and went off with the Secretary.

Ron was still inquisitive. “So, Station X is near Bedford?”

“No need for you to know where it is – but you and Joan did well. The code books are just what we need. Was there other information?”

Ron recapped on what he had learnt. “Wolfgang goes to Sweden to refresh the code books but also to do some listening and sending a series of messages for us to pick up. If we use direction finding to track the source of the signals, they appear to come from Scandinavia rather than Germany. He uses our recognition codes and systems to feed us information or should I say dis-information.”

Smith was astonished. “What! Our recognition codes? Are you sure this is right?”

Ron asked Nicholson, “Do your agents send regular reports back from Denmark and Norway?”

Smith and Nicholson were even more startled. Ron was not supposed to know about agents or even of their existence. After a second, Smith nodded to Nicholson.

“Yes they do.”

Ron corrected him. “No they don’t. They might come from the direction of Scandinavia, but Wolfgang is the one that sends them – from Sweden. Check the dates. I think you will find they are always sent when he is in Sweden. Your agents were captured as soon as they landed.”

Nicholson slammed his palms on the table. “Bugger. So they were either turned over or the codes were sweated out of them – poor souls.”

Smith was unhappy at this news to say the least. “We will check up. We’ll go back to the messages and see what stacks up. I suppose at least this means that our friend Schultze, assuming all this is true, is in a position to both send and receive messages from us.”

Ron confirmed this comment from Smith. “He is. He is going to tell us where and when we can find Hartmann and his team.”

“Where and when?” asked Smith. “What do you mean where and when?”

Ron explained what he had learnt in the short meetings with Schultze, building on what he had already known or surmised.

"Hartmann is trying to find our codebreaking team, although most of the German high command think he's up a gum tree. They're obsessed with the impregnability of their codes – what they see as the infallibility of the Enigma machine I imagine. If Hartmann finds our Station X they'll bomb it out of existence. So it's quite rational to him that we would do the same to his operation."

Nicholson sniffed. "As you know, he would be right."

Ron went on. "He has a novel solution to the risk of being attacked. They move their team, their base – they move it around in a special train."

Smith looked at Ron and Nicholson. "Sounds barmy. Hum, although it's an interesting idea."

Nicholson reflected for a moment. "Germany is a big country. It must make for logistical problems for their own side as well as making it harder for us to find them."

Ron filled in more details. "Hartmann likes the train. It's very plush apparently. The Kaiser used to use it. The perceived privilege is another reason for the jealousy and infighting with the other branches of the military and security establishment who don't much care for Hartmann. Anyway, they take the train round various towns. As well as presenting a moving target, it gives Hartmann a chance to keep in touch with other academics. As well as picking their brains he keeps up a social network."

Smith said, "Well I'll be blowed."

"How do we get dates from Schultze?" asked Nicholson.

Ron was on mathematical home ground. "He is going to send us the dates disguised in a message using prime numbers. Normally he sends messages out in groups of four letters or numbers in combination."

"That's quite true of the codes generally used by the Germans." Smith observed.

Ron checked. "And the message may have up to 50 or 60 such groups?"

"Yes."

Ron elaborated on the communication system he had devised with Schultze. "Tell our people to look for messages from our supposed agents in Scandinavia and to divide the stream of characters into groups of four, then to look at patterns in the groups that correspond to prime numbers. That's the second, third, fifth, seventh groups and so on. We can see what we get. We should be sending messages back to our agents, that we now know are not actually agents, to keep up the pretence, but I doubt we can have any effective two-way communication with Wolfgang."

*

Joan had everything organised for their trip back to the base. They had picked up their uniforms and given most of the civvy clothing back to the diplomatic service, although they had been allowed to retain some. Ron hoped this was not a signal that they would have to repeat some of the secret mission stuff. Joan might be cut out for it, but he wasn't. He had burnt a lot of nervous energy.

It had all been a bit of a whistle-stop tour, and the travelling of the last few days Ron had found a bit disorientating. They met the messenger in the lobby. The code books had been wrapped up into an anonymous looking package, which Ron noticed was addressed to Room 47 of the War Department. It looked like there was a need for a courier service from the London operation to Station X. A staff car took them the short distance across London from the offices to St Pancras station.

The messenger was a civilian, or seemed so. "The protocol is, Sir, we always take a first-class compartment in the train, the first one. It should be reserved for us. A car driver will meet the train at a station called Flitwick. He will come onto the train and meet us in the compartment. We do the handover there. Don't worry, the train won't leave the station until we have done the handover and he and I are off the train and make a signal to the guard."

If their package was so valuable, Ron wondered if the man was armed. Actually now he thought about it, he looked like a fit strong man. "So you will leave the train and go with the car driver. That way there's always at least two people with the package. And after that we just travel onto Leicester and Melton, I suppose."

"Yes sir. After I leave, your bit is done."

The staff car dropped them at St Pancras through the concourse and onto the platform as they moved against the throng of passengers coming the other way, as trains disgorged their passengers into the London terminus from the Midlands and north. Through the incoming flow of people they found their train. The messenger pointed out a coach. "After you Miss, Sir"

Joan edged down the corridor to the first class section. She pointed, "So, I think we should be in this compartment here – the one with the blinds down."

The messenger looked over her shoulder in the cramped space of the corridor. "That's right, this label is ours." He tapped on the glass where a there was a sticker showing the letters KM." Ron had passed the compartment door and turned and slid it open. It was already occupied.

Inside, there was an older naval officer and a rather attractive young lady. Ron guessed this was a man of senior rank – there was an awful lot of gold on his sleeves and shoulders. Ron wasn't very good at recognising RAF uniforms, so stood little chance with the Navy. An Admiral or Commodore maybe. Anyway, a lot higher rank than a RAF Flight Lieutenant.

The naval officer was dismissive, patronising even. "Would you mind? This compartment is taken."

Ron attempted to explain. "I'm afraid you must be in the wrong compartment, Sir. This one is reserved for us."

"Not any more it isn't. Get out and close the door."

Ron did not feel he wanted to get into a row, but it had been made clear that this compartment was the one where they would be met. "I really must insist sir – we have to have this compartment. It has been reserved for us."

The naval officer became annoyed. No doubt he was not used to having his words queried. And there was the added undercurrent of inter-service rivalry. The Senior Service versus the newest service – the RAF. "Who the hell do you think you are? Bloody fly boys trying to take over everything. Apparently no respecter of rank – clear out or your CO will be hearing about it."

The messenger edged past Joan and into the doorway. He held up a hand to Ron in a sort of 'let me handle this' gesture. Ron backed out of the congested space. The messenger spoke to the Admiral, or whatever he was. "Excuse me Sir. I am a King's Messenger – here is my warrant – the Flight Lieutenant is absolutely correct. There are reasons of security protocol that require us to occupy this compartment and I would respectfully ask you to allow us to use it."

The Navy man steadied the document in its leather wallet between his fingers as the messenger proffered it for examination. Even if he had never seen one before, he understood the authority it conferred on the bearer. He looked a bit nonplussed, but then in bluster gathered up his belongings and the girl.

"Come on m'dear." On the way out he snorted at Ron. "I'm prepared to be outranked by the King but not by the Royal Air Force – it's about time you fly boys knew your place."

Ron watched them move down the corridor and out of sight through the corridor connection into another coach. He joined the other two in the compartment and rolled the door closed. "That was a bit tricky- I never thought I'd be called upon to turf an Admiral out of his seat on the train."

The messenger shrugged. "Crowded trains – it sometimes happens. Though he seemed a bit sticky about it – more so than the once or twice it happened to me before. Mind you, never came across anybody so senior before."

Joan observed, "It may have been something to do with the company he was in. Do you think that was his niece?" She winked at Ron.

They settled down, stowing their stuff in the overhead racks, with Ron clutching the precious bag with the code books inside.

There was some slamming of doors and sound of whistles. There were other coaches on the next line. The windows of the other coach started to glide past, very slowly. After a second or two, the sensation of movement was resolved – an illusion – it was their own coach that was moving. A jerk on the couplings as the locomotive started to accelerate showed them it was their own train pulling out. The train cleared the platform and the station canopy, and a shaft of late afternoon sun lit up their compartment. The bark of the engine's exhaust echoed off London's buildings crowding around the railway line. Smoke-stained brick passed the window and soon became blurred and difficult to focus upon as the train gathered speed.

Ron enquired of the messenger, "Do you do many runs like this?"

The messenger was more forthcoming than might be expected. "Yes, I get to go to all sorts of places. Sometimes on my own, sometimes I have to be with someone else, like now. For this run I usually go from Euston to Bletchley."

"Really?" said Ron.

*

Events at Flitwick station went exactly as forecast. Another chap in civvies appeared at their compartment door. These two messengers presumably knew one another, as there did not seem to be any passwords or anything like that. Ron wondered if he had read too many novels. The first messenger relieved Ron of the bag with the codebooks, shook hands and wished them a good trip. Ron felt a sense of relief. As soon as the messengers were out of the corridor onto the platform the train was away again, slowly overtaking the two men as they strode along the platform.

Now Ron and Joan had the compartment to themselves for the rest of the trip. Something of a luxury as many trains were well up to capacity– and often beyond with standing room only, depending on the route and time of day. Joan moved round to sit opposite Ron. Her skirt hem rode up as she did so, showing a glimpse of stocking top as she sat down.

Ron commented, "Well – just you and I together again for a while. Someone told me that the appeal of the WAAF is the uniform with the stockings. I just got a glimpse of your stocking top there."

"Oh! You mean these!" She pulled up the hem again to reveal a better view of suspenders and stocking tops. "I wonder why it is that men cannot resist a glimpse of stocking."

Ron tried to speak with a coolness he did not feel. "Has to be the right pair of legs of course."

"And are mine the right pair of legs?"

"Certainly." Ron nodded and paused to glance out of the window at the steam drifting by across the open countryside. Joan's flirtations were difficult to ignore – not that he wanted to. "It was quite an experience in Stockholm -- wasn't it?

Joan was still teasing him. "Now what part of the experience are we talking about here?"

"Well – let's weigh up the score card – there was getting told of our trip at short notice, and getting kitted out in civvies from the super wardrobe of clothes that the diplomatic service seem to hold."

Joan agreed. "Yes, that was something."

Ron continued. "The flight to Sweden in the back of that Mossie. Something to look back on – especially since I was full of apprehension. Fearful of being travel sick, wondering if we could carry it off."

Joan said, "You didn't look worried – in fact I remember thinking you seemed calm and in control. Mind you, your air sickness on the way back wasn't the greatest part of the trip."

"Did I tell you I have some problem with my ears – apparently ears control one's sense of balance and such? That's why I'm not supposed to fly. That and my eyesight. You were quite understanding about it, I thought. Did I say thank you?"

Joan smiled. "Several times. You didn't need to though. We'd been through a lot – made us even closer I thought. So what else is there on the score card?"

"So I guess that leaves the fun of the chase with Wolfgang and …"There was a knock on the compartment door. Ron opened it and the train guard was outside.

"Sorry to disturb you Sir, miss. There was a message at the last station. There's an unexploded bomb on the line – it's the other side of Leicester. There'll be no trains through to Melton until tomorrow. I'm afraid you will have to sleep on the train or get a hotel in either Market Harborough or Leicester.

Ron said, "Oh… okay thanks." The door slid closed.

Joan raised her eyebrows. "Well, well, well. Here we all were, talking about our experience together in Sweden – let us say a shared experience, and it looks like we've got to go through it all again."

Ron responded, "I was just about to ask you how you rated – what shall we call it – how you rated the overnight experience."

"Let's put it this way. I can imagine hotel rooms will be at a premium in Leicester – I think we will have to share a room again – don't you?"

“Ah. The butterflies of excitement are back in my tummy again.”

Joan said, “Is that where they are?”

Chapter 10

After his trip abroad and the time in London, Ron found things much as he had left them at Whittingsmore. The key difference was the absence of Evans for most of the time – he was out training.

A day or two after his return, Ron was summoned to the Group Captain's office. Ryland started off by welcoming him back. "I hear excellent reports of your trip overseas. I don't know the details – don't need to. But well done."

Ron was glad he seemed to have lived up to expectations. "Thank you Sir. It certainly made a change from the regular job. Not that the job's been that regular for a while."

Ron found his boss Ryland considerably less aloof than their relative ranks might merit. Ryland gave Ron a bit of an update. "Now then – Evans has had a crash course in flight training; although I hope crash isn't the right word", he smiled and carried on "and as we speak he is doing target practice on the range. We've paired him up with a pilot – Sergeant Woodward. Although he's only a sergeant he's actually the best pilot for this job we think." Ryland may have had a second thought that he was demeaning the non-commissioned officers and made something of a retraction. "Though, sorry didn't mean to put it that way – you were only a sergeant until recently after all – and look at you."

Ron wasn't bothered at all. "Oh you don't need to worry about upsetting me, Sir. I've had an exciting time of late, but still takes a bit of getting used to when people start saluting."

Ryland proceeded. "Anyway, I gather Evans seems to be a natural. We are not teaching him to take off and land – he is just going to fly the Mossie during gun attack phase. As it happens Woodward is a trained navigator so we hope not to have to depend on any navigation skills from Evans. He is not being trained for that."

Ron now thought he had maybe been a bit rash suggesting Evans for this job. He had not expected Evans to be actually piloting the Mosquito, just translating from the Welsh speaking ground controller, for the pilot to line up the attack. Now Ron came to think about it, he could see that way of doing things would not be ideal. He decided to ask about Evans and his training progress before he next met Nicholson.

He wondered how much Ryland knew about the purpose of the intended op. He obviously was involved in organising the flying part of the task. "Do you know about the radio navigation aids, Sir?"

Apparently Ryland did know about 'Oboe'. "Yes. A box of tricks is being mounted in the Mossie tomorrow – you know some of our brass are not convinced about the system?"

Ron risked a critical comment. "Yes, but they weren't convinced about our high-speed Lancaster either."

Ryland made a sort of 'humph' sound. "Indeed not, however progress on that one too." Ryland looked as if he had a sense of amused satisfaction about the Lancaster with the damaged turret, Whisky Sugar. "She's been pulled ahead in a revised repair programme – the bits for the upper turret arrived last week and they had started work to refit it. But then this morning, I issued new work orders to leave it out and re-sheet and streamline the turret aperture. The Group Captain chuckled. "I am told Sykes wasn't too pleased when he heard."

Ron could well imagine the colourful language that would emanate from Sykes when he got orders like that and had a chuckle himself. "I'd like to have been there then, Sir!"

"We've got some up-rated Merlin's and we're working much harder to streamline the whole aircraft, rivets, skin treatment – that sort of thing. We're going to try and get every little bit of extra speed we can out of her. It's Nicholson's op and it's up to us to try and support as much as we can.

Ron was waiting for the sting in the tail with various tasks that might be asked from him. "Sounds like things are moving quickly, sir."

Ryland's orders were a bit more vague than Ron expected. Perhaps as a commissioned officer, that was the difference in how instructions were characterised. "As soon as you get the chance, go over and see Nicholson – I want you to keep on the case for this op – it all stems from your ideas."

Ron went over to the North hanger that afternoon. He found Frank Nash from the SOE team with Nicholson. They were looking at the Mosquito with the big gun which was residing in the hangar. Nash stood underneath the nose inspecting the protruding barrel and then they walked back together toward the office within the building, talking as they went. Ron asked, "So you've picked your man to be dropped into Belgium then?"

Ron knew that this would be one of the Welsh speakers selected from the 'interview sessions' in London.

Nicholson replied, "Yes, he is in the Royal Marines – a commando – all the candidates are good but he seemed to have the best aptitude – animal cunning and whatnot. Being a commando meant a shorter training time as well. He is a big strong man – he has to handle a heavy transmitter set powerful enough for a flying aircraft to be able to listen to his guidance from the ground. His Welsh is up to the mark. We are going to try and do the drop-in by parachute to the Belgian resistance and fly him out as soon as the show is over at Florennes. We certainly don't want him captured, although he is a tough man and I would back him to fight his way out of a corner. We are calling him by the codename 'Lion'. All he's got to do on this mission is talk in the attack so we can be sure we get our target."

They entered a doorway to the offices and went in to one of the rooms, pulling up chairs round the table.

Nicholson began, "So now you're here we can go over the plan. Ok?"

Ron and Nash nodded.

Nicholson produced a map from a locked cabinet in the corner. "We will have our man 'Lion' in position watching the Chateau. The Belgian resistance are very confident in the target's routine. Herr Bauer always dines about seven, often after some shenanigans with local girls who may or may not be compliant. He takes a bath and dresses for dinner – rather fancies himself as an aristocratic. This of course does mean we should know where he is. From the spinney just outside the estate you can see into the dining room with a pair of binoculars. Lion and the resistance will be camped there. When Evans and Woodward are ready for their attack in the mosquito, Lion will talk them in, watch impact of the shells and ensure that the target is eliminated."

Frank Nash was interested in the technology side, both theirs and ours. He pointed at the map and various installations and building that were marked. "The Mosquito then flies on to the radar station and bombs it. Both of these attacks within a couple of minutes of one another are going to have to be under visual guidance – in the case of the Chateau from the ground but the radar station is going to be up to the skill of the aircraft crew, particularly Woodward. Florennes is only about 100 miles from the coast – so this is not like a full scale attack on Hamburg."

Nash waved his hand about in a mimic of the approach of the aircraft "The setting sun will be behind the Mosquito's run in – we hope speed and accuracy as well as the twilight will provide sufficient protection from Jerry's air defence. As soon as we can arrange it afterwards, the Lancaster will arrive, under radar guidance from Oboe, I might add, so we hope to keep Dr James satisfied. It will drop a full stick of bombs on both the Chateau and then on the radar station. If we get Bauer, the agents will send the signal "Jericho" to signal a successful, er, elimination. It seemed an appropriate code word for knocking down walls."

Nicholson resumed. "We hope the Germans will think that the attack was directed at the radar station – which is after all a very valuable target. Immediately after the raid Nicholson will be sending in our Lysander to pick up Lion, we want him to be in enemy territory for as short a time as possible. Have we got everything in place from your side, Cooper?

Ron had done his homework since getting back and seeing Ryland. "Think so. Evans has turned out to be a star pupil on the training, accurate gunfire is quite possible in daylight as long as there is minimal opposition. The Lanc is ready to go and whilst it's not as fast as the Mossie, Florennes is close enough that we hope the defence response time is not quick enough to provide an interception before we can hit both targets. The Lanc bomb load will be quite something if we can confine it to a small area. We'll keep the lads training until you give us the go."

Nicholson said, "The time to go depends on two things – the target, Bauer being in the château and a suitable weather window. The resistance and our man Lion say that Bauer's routine is now well established, but we should go as soon as we can."

“So it’s all down to the weather then.” Ron rose from the table. “I’ll go round straight away and see Bob Neal, the Sergeant who looks after the met forecasts.”

*

Two days later the weather cleared and all was set. It was now a fine spring evening. There was a usual pre-flight briefing for the crew of the Lancaster, ‘Whisky Sugar’ and the team of Woodward and Evans in the special Mosquito. Nicholson sat silently in the corner, watching and listening. The Lancaster would take off first with the faster Mosquito a few minutes later. The tail gunner of the Lancaster might be expected to be a bit more nervous than usual with no upper turret. That, and a faster aircraft following on a similar heading, made for a risk of a friendly fire problem. Also they intended radio silence between the aircraft. Finally, it was the practice to try the guns over the sea with a short burst. The last thing they wanted was an accident and it would be up to Woodward to keep well clear of the big bomber.

As the crew left for the waiting aeroplanes, Ron clapped Evans on the back and spoke to him in Welsh, “Good luck Rhys – should be as easy as shooting foxes.”

Evans seemed excited more than fearful. “Thank you, Sir. Maybe not easy, but certainly more exciting. Goodbye.”

Having checked all round the aircraft – the customary walk round – Woodward climbed up into the Mosquito cockpit. He negotiated his way round the dual control stick on the starboard, co-pilot side of the cabin. There was not much room in the Mosquito cockpit normally, but this special one-off version with dual controls and the big gun made things even more congested. Rhys Evans followed him through the hatch and after the usual struggle to stow parachutes, dropped his bottom onto the seat. As he did so, they saw the Lancaster ‘Whisky Sugar’ in front of them dead ahead on the next dispersal pan, with one propeller starting to turn. The first of the four engines coughed into life, with a brief flurry of smoke and flame – a sequence repeated from the other three. The noise from the Lancaster vibrated the windows in the Mosquito. The big bomber slowly moved forward as the wheel chocks were pulled away. For a moment, Woodward and Evans stopped looking for seat belts and watched the bomber begin its progress to the runway. It turned broadside onto them, showing an unusual lateral profile with its missing turret. Woodward thought that it looked vulnerable without that protection and hoped that the bosses knew what they were doing.

Woodward did his pre-flight checks, and they were ready for engine start as Whisky Sugar swept down the runway and was lost from sight behind a hangar. They started their own engines, taxied out on to the runway and watched the stop watch tick round. Woodward had stuck it to the dashboard with chewing gum and tape. Normally, the navigator would have the watch, but as he was navigator and pilot on this mission, he wanted it where he could see. He liked Evans and was happy to have the addition of the electronic 'Oboe' navigation box, but it was early days to fully trust either with navigation.

Accurate time was the key element both for flying navigation generally and this mission specifically. Normally, finding a spot on the map involved flying at a known speed in a set direction, by compass heading, then using the time to work out the location, after allowing for wind. This time they had the Oboe kit to help get them there, but the whole thing was highly time dependent. They wanted to be over the château at a very specific time, to catch their target Bauer when they knew where he would be. They were faster than the Lancaster and would overtake it, flying at pre agreed speeds to co-ordinate their attacks. Take off time was critical.

After 90 seconds of idling at the end of the runway, Woodward was glad to see the time come up before overheating of the engines became an issue. Pushing the throttles forward, they quickly gathered speed and lifted off, just, Woodward hoped, like the training flights they had done. The flat, open fields of East Anglia rolled beneath the nose of the Mosquito, perfectly illuminated by the sun behind them. They stayed low, crossing the coast and glimpsing the Lancaster away to their port and much higher. As instructed and in the interests of self preservation, Woodward peeled off to starboard to follow his dog leg route to the target.

They kept radio silence until they crossed the Belgium coast at tree top height flashing past farms and observers, gone before anyone had a chance to react – that was the plan at least. Evans powered up the radio and addressed the microphone. *"Llew der i fewn.Romeo Victor.Romeo Victor yn galw."*[5]

There was a pause filled only with crackling. Evans readied to push the transmit button again, but through the static, a Welsh voice came across the airwaves. As in all the practice runs, it was incomprehensible to Woodward, but he had learned that 'Llew, Llew, Llew' meant 'Lion, Lion, Lion.'

Even more so than radio transmissions from the air, the possibility of detection of the source by the enemy was a looming fear. Keeping communications as short as possible was the plan. Evans listened intently to the voice from the ground. *"Llew, Llew, Llew. Mae pobeth yn barod. Mae'r targed yn ei le."*[6]

Evans acknowledged with some Welsh words that Woodward guessed meant some sort of confirmation. Evans pointed to the box and then the watch and shouted, "How long?"

---

5 *"Lion come in. Lion come in. Romeo Victor. Romeo Victor calling."*

6 *"Lion. Lion. Lion. Everything is ready. Target is in place."*

Woodward tapped the Oboe navigation box then pointed to the watch and held up three fingers. "The magic box tells us three minutes. Open bomb doors."

Switching back to Welsh, he responded to Lion "Three minutes."

Lion crackled back "Begin tracer as soon as you sight target." During the practice they had decided to fire a burst of tracer to help sight the big gun. Otherwise the ground observer had no idea where the gun was pointing."

Woodward cut in, "Open the bloody bomb doors!"

Suddenly there was much to do in a short time. Evans had not forgotten the bomb doors in rehearsals. "Oh yes sorry – forgot, yes bomb doors opening."

Evans resumed his Welsh on the radio. *"Dylswn fod yno mewn dwy funud – sefwch gerllaw.*[7]

Woodward gained some altitude and slowed the speed over the ground. The Mosquito's high speed was an asset in getting them there without harassment from air or ground defences, but they needed time to align the guns – tracer and the Molins cannon. As soon as they started firing, the recoil forces would slow the aeroplane. In practice they had found there was a balance between risking too slow a speed to successfully control against the recoil – and having enough time for an accurate shot, under guidance from the ground controller.

At the top of the climb they could see further. The lighting was better than even they hoped, for there, illuminated by the setting sun and almost dead ahead, was a white dot surrounded by green trees. With its whitewashed walls the château stood out, as if in a spotlight.

---

7 *"Should be there in two minutes – standby."*

*

Lion and a man called Lambregts had been hunkered down in a spinney about 150 metres away from the back of the Château. Lion's insertion into occupied Belgium had followed the usual SOE pattern – a night parachute drop met by the Belgium resistance. Lion had never used a parachute before his recruitment for this job, but had survived two practice drops, and the real thing, unscathed. Lambregts had looked after Lion for the past two days and guided him to the hidey hole they had now. Lambregts thought he spoke good English, but did have trouble understanding Lion from time to time. Nevertheless they got by and had observed the comings and goings at the château, which followed a routine pattern as the intelligence had suggested. This evening, they had a clear view of a terrace and beyond it could see through glazed doors into what seemed through the binoculars, to be a dining room. It was centrally located under a balcony to a bedroom. Tonight, Bauer was apparently entertaining another officer. They stepped out onto the terrace and Bauer was making expansive gestures over the view of the countryside and the spinney from where they watched. Crowing over his acquisition of the property, no doubt. They were watched as they enjoyed a cigarette and after a while, their return to the dining room.

Lion and Lambregts could not make out details in the room, but with the dining table placed near the window the figures could be seen to be seated and commencing their meal. Lion checked his watch and turned on the bulky radio set he had lugged out to their vantage point. He donned headphones. They waited and watched. Right on time, Evans' voice, the voice he heard before over the telephone and in practices, could be made out in his headphones, with the din of an aircraft cockpit as a background. He, like Woodward in the Mosquito, held up three fingers to Lambregts. They both stared intently through their field glasses. Everything was set, but Lambregts concerned himself about the two Belgian servants retained by the Nazi in the Chateau. They had been warned to stay in the kitchen pantry at this time, but whether this would offer sufficient protection in the oncoming havoc no one knew. They had bravely turned up for work as usual though, to avoid any possibility of suspicions being aroused. The minutes and seconds ticked by. Lion made short, incomprehensible utterances into the radio. They waited.

Unable to hear the radio, Lambregts listened for the sound of an aircraft whilst staring unblinkingly at the diners through the binoculars. Carried on the slight breeze between the sounds of the birds and a humming crackle leaking from the radio set, he fancied he heard something. Lion was working the radio and spoke a few short sharp words. Now Lambregts was sure he could hear the distant drone of an aeroplane. At once the presence of the attacker was made clear. Over their heads and above the trees, a stream of tracer whooshed towards the building. It pitted the ground, drew sparks from the iron balustrades and smashed windows in the room to the right of the dining room. Lion was barking more instructions into the radio.

Though the glasses Lambregts could see a startled Bauer rise and turn to the window. With grim satisfaction, Lambregts could now see a man – his enemy who he hated with a vengeance – a man about to die. A second burst of tracer drove straight into the glazed doors. The view of Bauer was lost in a hail of glass shards, sparks and dust. A second later a sheet of orange flame filled his whole view and he dropped the binoculars. The sound of explosions reached them. It was one muffled bang after another in quick succession all centred on the same spot. Rubble was being thrown in all directions. The dark shadow of the Mosquito that was the instrument of Bauer's doom, flashed over their heads at treetop height, then straight over the target. Lambregts thought it was going to slice the roof off the building, and as soon as it arrived, it was gone, obscured by the dust cloud. The sound of the engines roared after it was lost from sight.

It had been five or six seconds of stunning, frenetic activity. Neither man said anything nor moved for a moment. The dust masking the building from view was beginning to settle. They raised their binoculars. The outline of the house was intact, including Lambregts noted with relief, the kitchen area. A smoking chasm had replaced of the middle part of the chateau where the dining room had been.

Lion and Lambregts faced one another. They said "Jericho!" in unison. Lion transmitted the code word through the radio, and then swiftly shut down the set.

*

In the Mosquito, Evans had taken over the stick at the top of long shallow dive toward the target. The value of rehearsals came home during the attack. They had done it so many times that it was instinct, fitting in all the actions in a short space of time: coordinating with the ground controller whilst firing tracer and the big gun. The difference came as they passed close over the damaged château through a cloud of debris. In the practice runs they had only to knock out wooden profiles. As they swept through the cloud of dust and smoke there was a clattering as bits of château fell back to earth. They burst through the smoke and out into clear air the other side.

Evans shouted, "What was that?"

Woodward had control back and mentally checked the stability of the aircraft. "Debris – but she's still flying. Check bomb release for next target." There was no time to do other than continue the run straight on to the radar station. Within seconds the radar station hove into view. The radar antennae grids and lattices marked it out. Flying low over treetops from the coast the German radar only stood a chance of picking them up as they gained altitude for the attack, but if the defences hadn't been warned by their own radar kit, they would have heard the commotion from the château. As they lined up, bomb doors already open, they saw some figures running to gun outpost on the perimeter of the compound. It was a sprint that the gunners were bound to loose, the three gun installations were set in a radius about 70 yards from the main buildings. They let their bombs go in a stick, from low level, then Woodward opened the throttles wide and climbed away, before any firing rose from the ground.

Now there was a chance for a quick damage assessment. Woodward checked the gauges and Evans peered at the wings and engines. As far as they could tell the airframe was undamaged from the encounter with the debris cloud.

"Let's have a look shall we?" Woodward was already banking the aircraft to look back at the radar station. The rising smoke showed that at least one bomb had hit the main building, but the rest made a row of craters leading across the ground. Woodward was conscious that the Lancaster was due to show up in matter of minutes, although at a higher altitude, and more likely to have been detected as it made its approach. He wanted to give the Lanc crew the best chance they could. He calculated there was time for a strafing run to deter the gunners without getting entangled in the Lancaster's attack. They turned the Mosquito back and made a second low level pass, lining up two of the three gun emplacements. They emptied the magazines at the ground guns, in a sustained burst, hoping that the Lancaster would be unmolested. They turned for home at full throttle and low level without sticking around to see what happened next.

*

The Lancaster crew were flying by instruments, according to orders. They were to deliver a report at debrief on the operation of the Oboe box. As they approached the target, smudges of smoke could be seen rising from two spots on the countryside ten thousand feet below.

They stuck to their orders flying a steady slight curving course. The bomb aimer stared at the Oboe indicator, instead of his usual task to look at the ground through an optical bomb sight. His thumb hovered over the release button. The instant the special electronic equipment inside the Oboe set indicated the release point, the bomb aimer duly responding to its bidding. He squeezed the bomb release button.

The bomber lurched upward as it unloaded its cargo of bombs. Almost as soon as the bombs were gone, they saw a line of tracer lazily rising towards them. The guns had neither the accuracy, nor the altitude to reach the aircraft, but the pilot turned for home and away from the target as the bomb doors closed. Having evaded interception on the way in, the return leg was where they might expect unwanted company. As they neared the coast, the tail gunner saw a glint in the sky behind them and reported it to the captain. "Keep your eyes peeled" was the instruction. A few moments later it was obvious that they were being tailed. There were two interceptors closing on them, but the presumed hostile aircraft were not gaining as quickly as usual – the special bomber had that slight speed improvement. It was a dash for home airspace in the fading light. The pilot set the engines to boost, but still the presumed hostiles gained. There was a flicker from the leading interceptor – he was firing. As with the ground guns, the tracer showed that guns did not quite have the range. It was time to deter them. The rear gunner let rip in the hope that his Brownings might deter the fighters. They were now out over the sea – how close would they get? The tail gunner called out the situation to his pilot. The captain responded by putting the Lancaster into a dive that might give them an extra few knots, but if they ran out of height, they would be in trouble. At 5000 feet and mid channel, a final ineffective burst of gun fire from the inceptors signalled the end of the abortive chase. The attackers turned away and disappeared into the gathering gloom as the sun dropped below the horizon.

Chapter 11

After the attack, Lion and Lambregts made their way across fields and through woodlands in the direction of Florrenes. They had heard a series of explosions a matter of minutes or so after watching the demolition of the Chateau. Five or six minutes later they heard gunfire – the continuous rattle of anti-aircraft gunfire – but they had seen no aircraft. Then there was a series of loud explosions – huge percussions which were both heard and felt, shaking their bodies and the ground. A column of smoke rose in the gathering twilight. The sounds came from the direction they were headed.

Lambregts led the way to a farm track between trees, where a horse and cart was loosely laden with silage was waiting for them. Two bicycles were leaning against the cart and the horse was held by a boy of about 14 or 15, who was trying to calm the horse, which unsurprisingly, had been discomforted by the noise. Lambregts and Lion secreted the bulky radio under the load in the wagon after wrapping it an oilskin. Satisfying themselves that the radio was fully concealed underneath the pile, they looked around. They did not have long to wait, as, two men appeared through the trees, within a few minutes. Lambregts shook their hands and spoke in terms that were obviously an introduction for Lion. Lambregts explained that these were resistance people who had been watching the attack on the radar control station. They handed two small pieces of paper to Lion, who, as he had been instructed, concealed them in a compartment in the heel of his left shoe.

It was now nearly dark. Lambregts and Lion said goodbye to the boy and the two other men, and they took the bicycles to ride through the gathering gloom along back lanes. They saw no traffic, but could hear a commotion across the countryside, where no doubt, the rescue services of the occupying forces were busying themselves with the aftermath of the attack at the two sites. There was a glow in the night sky.

Eventually they came to a railway line and followed it until they came alongside a goods train that was stopped in a siding. On the other side of the train was a small goods yard. Lambregts dismounted and propped his bicycle against a line-side hut. He indicated for Lion to wait. Lion watched as he walked alongside the wagons. Reaching the head of the train, he was silhouetted in the glow from the fire of the engine. Lambregts half mounted the steps and had a brief conversation with the crew, who were out of Lion's sight. After a minute he walked back to Lion to fetch him. The pair clambered up onto the engine footplate where the driver and fireman were eating bread and cheese, and a smell of coffee mingled with the other smells of coal dust, oil and steam. There was a coffee pot perched on a shelf above the fire hole. "These men will take you to another handover", Lambregts explained. "They are waiting to add some more wagons and then the train will run through the night, crossing the border into France. I'm sorry they do not speak any English, but you will be met by someone from the French Resistance before dawn tomorrow."

This was Lion's exfiltration plan. As much as possible, SOE wanted to avoid an evidence trail linking to the Belgian Resistance and especially SOE's own involvement. By taking Lion across the border to France to the Pas de Calais area, even if caught, it was hoped there would be no connection with the raid of which he had been an intrinsic part. A further protection, it was hoped, was afforded by Lion's wearing of both his Royal Marine dog tags and tunic underneath his workman's overcoat.

If apprehended, particularly near the coast, he might appear to be an escaping British Serviceman.

Lambregts shook hands with Lion and the enginemen, spoke a few words and was gone. In the unlikely event of a check on the train and engine crew, Lion was to hide on the coal in the tender, hoping the darkness would prevent discovery.

More wagons were added to the rear of the train. Although neither driver nor fireman spoke English, they called Lion 'Tommy' and managed with sign language, sharing some of their supper with him. Lion repaid them by shovelling coal into the fire hole, when the time came to build up steam. Within an hour, a signal released the train from its siding and they clattered across the quiet Belgian countryside. After a bit more helping with stoking, Lion lay down to sleep amongst the coals in the tender. Despite the discomfort, he slept soundly, until the fireman shook him into consciousness and indicated it was time to go. He awoke to find that the train had stopped.

Lion roused himself and brushed coal dust from his clothes. It was still dark and there was another man climbing the steps onto the footplate. He greeted the driver and fireman, shaking hands. Turning to Lion, he said in perfect English, "So, you are the Lion, I am the Fox – my name is Reynard. Welcome to France." Although his English was perfect, the accent was very French. Reynard had a very friendly conversation in French with the footplate men. The liaison bore all the hallmarks of a routine communication system. They bade the engine crew farewell, climbed down the steps and walked alongside the train towards some buildings. Lion now saw that they were in a marshalling depot of some sort. They must be near a village because Lion heard a distant clock strike four o'clock. They entered a small brick building at the edge of the track. "This is an overnight hostel for train crews. We should be safe here". Reynard confirmed that he had regular contact with the same train crew. "But I won't be seeing them for a while; I am coming back to England with you."

They used the back stairway to an upper room. "This hostel is used for comings and goings at all sorts of hours, especially for train crews on night shifts. We will stay here tomorrow during the daytime, so you are not seen, and leave tomorrow night. We can try to get some sleep." Turning the light on, he looked at Lion, "You look like a railway man!" Lion was black from head to toe covered in coal and soot from the engine.

The room was windowless, except for a small level skylight covered by a curtain, from which a tall man like Lion could just about peer out. Lion slept fitfully during the day despite, or perhaps because of, his ability to sleep on the coal the preceding night. There was the constant sound of train movements and shunting outside and from time to time, he discreetly peered over the edge of the skylight to watch the activity. He tried to understand, without much success, the two or three French newspapers that were lying around. Reynard translated some of them for him. Time hung heavily as they waited for darkness.

When night fell, they left the hostel and walked about a mile or two alongside the railway lines. The footpath then diverted away from the railway and turned into a wider track, which they followed for a further two or maybe three miles. They seemed to be well away from any human habitation. In the darkness Lion's eyes gradually became accustomed to the open countryside, lit by a half moon occasionally obscured by cloud. The area seemed to be flat with low hedges and free of woodland or large trees. Reynard said, "We are here." The track crossed an open field disappearing beyond vision in the darkness. He pointed down the track. "This is our runway."

Reynard produced a battery torch and four paraffin lamps. He also had some small logs wrapped in cloths that had been dowsed in creosote. In the light of the torch they checked the time. Ten minutes to midnight. They walked down the track for 150 yards, checking for obstructions.

Reynard returned back up the track having placed the paraffin lamps at each end of their improvised runway. They scattered the cloth-wrapped logs at intervals along the track. A few minutes past midnight, they heard a single engine aircraft and lit the lamps and the rags along the track. SOE's Lysander made a sharp and short landing, pretty impressive flying even for a small slow aircraft. Reynard and Lion stood at each end of the track next to the paraffin lamps. The aircraft stopped well short of Lion and turned and taxied back towards Reynard. The pilot would turn the aircraft when it reached Reynard and take off in the same direction it had landed. All they needed to do was to collect the paraffin lamps leaving the logs to burn themselves out and jump aboard.

*

The four German patrol men had a rather overlarge open backed lorry at their disposal, which proved useful in requisitioning cases of wine from local hostelries. After an eventful evening, they had consumed a few too many bottles of best French wine and succeeded in getting lost in the French countryside. The driver and Corporal in charge were not worried about getting back too late – their Commanding Officer had been recalled for some briefing or other and the other NCO's were very happy with the booty usually retrieved on their forays to improve the cellar in the German barracks.

Through an alcoholic haze the driver turned the lorry onto a country track and stopped to relieve the pressure on his bladder. His companion in the cab was asleep and the other two soldiers were sitting on the open flat bed facing backwards, leaning on the rear of the cab. They were singing in a drunken fashion. The

Corporal, having brought the truck to a halt, turned the cab light on, opened the door and climbed down for his pee. He stood against the open cab door and started to relieve himself. He then noticed a burning paraffin lamp some distance from where he was standing. Odd. He looked around. Above the sound of his lorry engine idling, and the carousing of his colleagues in the back of the lorry, he heard another engine. He looked down the track ahead of the lorry. Fancying he saw movement, he leaned into the cab and turned the lights onto full beam. There in the headlights was a sight that took time to assimilate. An aircraft was slowly turning, taxiing round. As it turned, British roundel markings could be seen on the side of the fuselage. The shock permeated his addled brain. "Mein Gott!" he shouted. He reached into the cab and shook his sleeping companion. The singing from the flatbed above and behind him abruptly stopped as he banged on the planked side of the lorry and turned back to face the aircraft. It was the last movement of his life. A commando's knife buried itself into his throat and Lion lowered the man to the ground as he fell dead. The nearest soldier in the back of the lorry leaned over the side planks extending his arm with a pistol in his hand. Lion grabbed the wrist, pulled the arm over the side and stabbed into the armpit under the outstretched arm. The grip on the pistol loosened and Lion prised the weapon from his fingers. In the dim light he took but a second to examine the gun and turn it to point at the struggling soldier leaning over the side of the truck and shot him in the face at point blank range. Turning, Lion fired two shots into the man seated in the cab next to the driving seat, before he had a chance to react. The second soldier in the back stood and picked up a machine gun, leaned over the side and sprayed automatic fire in the general direction of the big commando. Lion fired back at the muzzle flashes.

Reynard had run the length of the truck from the Lysander, a gun in his hand. From the light of his torch he examined four dead soldiers scattered around the lorry with its engine still idling. Lion was slumped on the cab steps, alive but in a bad way. "Have you been hit?" Lion grunted in reply. Reynard took the German pistol from Lion's hand, and threw it on the ground. He retrieved the Commando's knife that was lying at the feet of one of the corpses and kept it. He wanted to remove the evidence. Instead, he pulled a bayonet from the belt of one of the German corpses and smeared it across the blood stained clothes and then threw that on the ground. He turned off the lorry lights and stopped the engine. He ran over to the two paraffin lamps and kicked them away from the track and into the field. He returned and helped Lion to his feet and the two staggered back down the track to the Lysander. It seemed to take an age, and Reynard knew that the pilot would be getting anxious to go. At the door of the aircraft they struggled to get the semi-conscious Lion into the cabin. As the door closed the pilot pushed open the throttles. In the faint light of the cabin instruments, Reynard could see that both he and Lion were covered in blood. Gathering speed, the Lysander bumped down the track and into the air, clearing the truck by inches, as they rose into the night sky.

*

As was normal, the RAF flight crews had been debriefed when they returned to the base on the day of the attack.

Damage to the Mosquito testified that Woodward and Evans had had a close call with debris thrown up as the Chateau had been hit. There were a large number of pockmarks over the aircraft, but due to its wooden construction these could be rectified to return it to full serviceability in a few days. Evans had reported receiving the codeword from the ground controller Lion, which seemed to suggest that the target had been eliminated. After attacking the radar control station, the return trip to the English coast had been uneventful, whereupon they were on the receiving end of some inaccurate gunfire from the British coastal defences. Aircrews had a system for dealing with this eventuality – they were provided with a Very pistol and different coloured flares.

The pistol could be fired out of a window or a special hatch and the colours were changed regularly, so that ground defenders would be able to identify friendly aircraft. On this occasion, it was an unusual time for a friendly aircraft to be returning and there had to be sharp work from Evans to fire the Very pistol with the correct recognition colours of the day. The gunnery ceased immediately the flares were seen, and Evans radioed a warning to the Lancaster which was following them home to be ready with their recognition signals. Quite how many returning aircraft were lost to fire from their own side was something not known to the flying crew, but they all knew it was a substantial danger, particularly to those often coming back after a fatiguing night-time attack deep into Germany. It seemed a particularly galling way to lose an aircraft and crew.

The Lancaster crew reported their attempted interception and how they attempted to outrun the attackers. There was debate about the extent to which they had had lucky escapes, and the contribution of the extra speed of the specially converted aircraft.

Three days after the attack, the SOE team gathered to assess what had happened and what they might learn. Ron approached the meeting feeling that the raid had been largely successful. Both aircraft had returned, and as far as he knew Bauer had been killed in the attack on the Chateau, basing his thoughts on the knowledge that the codeword had been received. He was also aware that the Lysander had been sent out and returned with someone, so that sounded as if it had gone okay as well.

When Ron arrived in the SOE meeting room in the North hangar, he found that Smith had journeyed up from London and was there with Nicholson. They all knew about the debrief from the flight crews. They gathered round the table and Nicholson started speaking. "As you know, we got all the aircraft back from Belgium, and that there was some superficial damage to the Mosquito, but the gun is okay and the aircraft is fixable, but we do need to think about tactics for this sort of low-level attack in future." He paused and the other two men nodded.

Ron said "That part of it has been successful then, but do we have more detail on the results – did they do the job?"

Nicholson said, "There's a man in the other room – he's from the French resistance. He came back in the Lysander sent to pick up the man Lion. Monsieur Reynard can tell us a bit about what went on, but only indirectly. He wasn't in Belgium and he does not know about our mission. So I want to call him in, but we want to listen. He does not need to know what we are about, so be careful with your comments".

Ron asked the obvious question. "I thought the idea was that Lion would tell us what happened himself. Where does this chap – Reynard did you say – where does he fit it?"

"Lion did not make it I'm afraid, but the good news is that he wasn't captured – he was killed and we retrieved his body."

Ron was shocked "Good news? What sort of good news is that?"

Smith chipped in. "Look Ron. The stuff we do isn't always clean – it was important that Lion wasn't taken. We want our Welsh-speaking idea – your Welsh-speaking idea – kept from the enemy as long as possible. If the Germans looked like taking him alive we would have tried to kill him ourselves. It may be shocking to you – but that's the way things are."

There was an uncomfortable silence for a second or two.

Nicholson got up. "Let's find out some details – I'll bring Reynard in." He left the room and could be heard having a short conversation with someone just out of sight. He returned accompanied by a man in his thirties dressed in dark clothes with dark hair. He had a dapper air about him, although there were signs of fatigue around his eyes.

Nicholson introduced him to the others. Reynard spoke excellent English, with a marked French accent. Nicholson asked Reynard to describe the experiences of the past couple of days and in particular what he had learnt from Lion.

Reynard narrated events. "After I met Lion, we hid for a full day in a room in a railwayman's hostel. We were together for most of that time. Although it's a good idea not to talk too much about the jobs, Lion was pleased with the mission he was on. He thought everything had gone absolutely according to plan. Otherwise, we just talked about other normal things, family life, upbringing and so on, comparing la France with les Pays de Galles – Wales you call it."

Reynard went on to give an account of the problems at the pick-up in the French field – how they had been discovered by the German patrol and how Lion had killed them all. Smith and Nicholson were keen to find out if the German patrol had been specifically looking for this pick-up, which would indicate that their network had been compromised. Alternatively, was this a patrol systematically searching the area because there had been a more general suspicion that British agents and the resistance had been active there?

Reynard ventured an opinion. "I think it was just bad luck. It was difficult to see what was going on, in the dark and with all the action, but it didn't look like an organised patrol. They had quite a few cases of wine in the lorry, and the whole thing smelt of drink. I think these Germans had been out......?"

"Out on the town?" said Ron.

"Yes – out on the town. Some, but not all, of the German units get very relaxed about their posting in France. No, I don't think they were looking for us. They weren't ready, and made no attempt to creep up on us. My guess is we saw them first."

Smith posed a question. "You have some idea how the Germans work in occupied France. What will they make of it when they find their lorry in a field full of dead soldiers?"

Reynard made a Gallic gesture of spreading his hands. "Well of course I would be guessing. I tried to make sure we left no evidence behind – I picked up the knife of Lion and of course we brought him out in the plane, although he died on the way. We could do nothing for him."

Smith asked, "Wouldn't there be wheel marks in the field from the aeroplane?"

"Maybe, but the weather has been dry and the aeroplane uses a small road – a track you would call it. If they make a big search of the fields they might find a couple of tin lamps I used to mark the landing runway, but I kicked these away out into the field. They were all shot with their own weapons, although whoever is investigating might wonder about the stab wounds."

Nicholson summarised. "So our best guess, and our hope I should add, is that a group of partying German soldiers stumbled across you and Lion – and our Lysander. They were as surprised as you were."

Smith added, "And we also have to hope that the German investigation will assume this is the outcome of a drunken brawl between their own soldiers on an illicit night out."

"I will go back to France soon. We will have to be more careful and not make any operations in that area for a while. We will just have to wait to see what the Nazis will do. If they suspect something, we will know. They will start searching homes and arresting anyone they think might know something. If it stays quiet – it must be they think it an incident of poor discipline among their own troops."

"You look like you need a rest" said Nicholson. "Thanks for all you're doing. We'll get someone to take you to a billet and get you a good meal."

Reynard laughed at the expense of his hosts. "A good meal in England – that's a joke! Even before the war when I was here, I never came anywhere near a good meal. My friends, when the war is over, come to France and we will show you how to cook!" He slapped Nicholson on the back as they got up to see him out.

After Reynard left the office, they watched him through the glass wall of the offices as he walked across the hangar floor, escorted by one of Nicholson's men. Ron sighed, "There goes a brave man, going back having only just made a getaway last time."

Smith said, "Meanwhile, what do we think – I can see no reason that this will affect our plans? "

Ron noted to himself that the two SOE men saw the loss of their man Lion as an unemotionally tied incident of fact. He then mentally pulled himself up. Surely he had been the same when he broke the news that the British agents that SOE had thought were still at large, had been captured and turned over – the information he had got from Schultze in Sweden. Ron felt the loss of Lion more, as it was as a result of his decisions and ideas that the Royal Marine came onto their team in the first place. Now he was gone. Ron left this thought behind to listen to the continuing conversation.

Nicholson agreed that there was nothing to do but carry on, in the absence of evidence of any breakdown in their security. "As things stand, and despite losing one man, the raid was a big success. The flyers all came back – we hit both targets. Bauer in the chateau was a definite witnessed kill and the radar station is out of action."

Smith added a bit more information. "Most important of all, Jerry thinks the château was collateral damage. We've been monitoring the radio intercepts, and they are sure the radar station was the target."

Nicholson expressed a grim satisfaction. "So the concept has been proved."

Smith spread out two crumpled sheets of paper. "These were recovered from Lion – he had them hidden on his body. They were given to him by the Belgian resistance. They show where the bombs actually fell whilst they were watching the raid. They must have got these diagrams to Lion within a very short time after the raid. Goodness knows how they did it."

Ron read some notes at the bottom of the page that were written in French. "Paced out from known landmarks." The little maps showed the buildings sketched out and several marked craters that must represent the fall of the sticks of bombs. "They seemed to have planned well."

"Dr James will be pleased. The bombing was done by Oboe guidance – so this mission has proved the accuracy of that system thanks to the Belgian patriots. James will be happy with the accuracy, as well as the radar control station hit."

Nicholson was thinking ahead. "How is your man Evans?"

Ron had spoken to him. “Evans is a sort of shaken hero. His first op of course. I suppose we can avoid telling him about Lion – after all it was just a voice over the radio to him.”

Nicholson replied, “We need to keep him on the straight and level – he did a good job and we need him to keep in practice for the next op. The top priority now is Hartmann and for that strike we have to fly all the way to Germany.

Chapter 12

Schultze had returned to his post with the coding team, after his latest trip to Sweden. He found that his desk, which when he had left was in Regensburg in Southern Germany, had now moved to Würzburg with the mobile coding unit based in Hartmann's special train. Never mind the British finding them; it was hard enough for the staff to find the train. Either Hartmann thought it was some sort of initiative test not to tell Schultze when they were moving, or he just couldn't be bothered to keep a minion informed about a change of plan, while Schultze had been in Scandinavia.

Having found the location, Schultze was due to check back with Hartmann. He tried to keep his contacts with his boss, for whom he had an intense dislike, to a minimum. Hartmann had a whole carriage allocated to him, which was appointed with unabashed luxury. He found Hartmann at his desk in a swivel chair, with a uniformed SS soldier in attendance. Hardly had Schultze got through the door than the Prof started speaking, even before he had swivelled round to face him. "So you threw our codes books away – and made a hash of that."

Unsurprisingly, a report of his trip had preceded his arrival, but getting a dressing down was nothing new for Schultze or indeed anyone on the team. "I obeyed the orders, Herr Professor. We, we were under attack and….."

Professor Hartmann affected an exasperated and patronising tone. "Well at least we know they were destroyed, but you panicked – and was it necessary to pull a gun on the captain?"

Schultze attempted a defence. "He was starting to examine the papers."

Hartmann waved his hand to silence his junior. "If it wasn't for your crass action the situation need not have arisen. Thank God your technical work is better than your silly actions when undertaking a simple errand." He sighed, and then changed the subject, "Still we have vital work to do for the Reich. I propose to move the train to minimise the risk of the English finding us. I have set up a new movement timetable"

Schultze wondered if the higher authorities were thinking that Hartmann was a bit paranoid about being detected. A few of the others in the coding team, who got moved around the country, thought he was over-obsessed. In fact probably most of them did. Schultze of course, knew that his Professor's assumptions were more accurate that even Hartmann himself feared. "Do you think they are looking for us Herr Professor?"

"We are looking for them; surely they must be looking for us. When we find them we will destroy their capability to even attempt to penetrate our communications." Hartmann launched off into a tirade. He might be clever – brilliant even – but he was a Nazi bigot. He gave Schultze and the SS man the dubious benefit of his opinions. "The English have become degenerate. We know many Poles, Slavs and Jews went to England, some stealing our learning from our German universities. I suspect some of them are working in code-breaking. Do you remember when we went to England? They even had a Jewish student at my seminars – the cheek of it. No – they must be dealt with."

Schultze tried to lead the conversation in a different direction. "You are sure they can read some of our signals?"

"Some? Well maybe. If not now, in a while. Science has a way of finding an answer to every innovation in time. The fools at the Wehrmacht are convinced the Enigma machine is infallible. At the least the Kriegsmarine has up-rated theirs – I suspect the naval one is now practically impossible to break – at least for some years. The coding combinations are huge – tens of millions to one. But my theory is that if you can make a machine to code something you can make one to decode it. If so, they may be able to penetrate Wehrmacht signals at some point."

Hartmann recited his reasoning, reasoning that Schultze had heard before. Possibly Hartmann was subconsciously re-convincing himself every time he went through the explanation – reassuring himself against his critics. "The Wehrmacht may think I'm mad to keep moving about to avoid attack – but what do they know? In the meantime we keep moving."

"This is our movement plan for the next three months. After Leipzig we go to München, then Strassburg, then back to Hamburg. We can check on the work of the academics at the universities in these places. As well as good work – I will expect to be properly wined and dined by the University wherever we go." He shuffled some papers on his leather-bound desk and produced a list of towns which he handed to Schultze. "You had better make the arrangements with the railway people for the next move.

Schultze took the list. "Yes, Herr Professor."

The uniformed SS man was keeping notes of some sort. Hartmann kept Schultze standing while continuing the interview from his chair. "What's happening with your attempts to test if they are reading our messages?"

Schultze recapped, although he would have thought the Prof already knew all this. "I send messages out, purporting to come from their agents – the ones we captured – and try to work out if they are replying. Sometimes they do, sometimes not. I think they must rely on some of the BBC bulletins, rather than replying straight back or at set times. The information I have does not give me the full details on how the reply should work."

"Such as it is, the information that came from the captured British agents may be unreliable." Hartmann was callous about the enemy agents they had captured. "Pity the swine died under torture before telling us the whole story about how it works."

Schultze added, "I also send out messages which are random collections of letters and numbers in groups. It's a sort of control case." As a scientist and academic Hartmann should agree the benefit of effectively random control cases to help confirm that any messages in reply were genuine responses and that communication was working. Schultze also wanted to be able to send just what he liked for his own purposes.

Hartmann indicated that the discussion was ended, by an impatient wave from the back of his hand. "Don't bother me with details; let me know when you have something important."

*

Following the raid on Belgium and the earlier trip to Sweden, Ron's involvement with the SOE team went into a lull. There was going to be a period of waiting. Until they received coded messages from Wolfgang Schultze, they would have no idea what the next steps might be on disrupting the German coding and decoding operations. He caught up with administrative matters on the base. Joan too was back to dealing with various personnel issues around the Group. Ron had found her an off-base billet, which was a tiny farm-workers cottage, about a mile from the gate. Prior to the Swedish trip, she had used a room which backed onto the boiler house-block. This was a cosy and warm spot in the winter months in the middle of the base. Now she had more duties off-base rather than at Whittingsmore, driving herself round the other six aerodromes in the Group , for which the RAF had provided her with a car. There was another reason – discretion. Neither Ron nor Joan wanted to parade their relationship in full view of everyone and Ron coming and going to Joan's accommodation on the base would be a potential problem. Ron reflected on the perception of morality in wartime Britain. Extra-marital love-making was bad; scheming all day to kill other human beings was broadly good, as long as they were the enemy. Actually, Ron had no compunction about fighting the war – with his inside knowledge of atrocities he could see it was a matter of the greater good to defeat Nazi Germany and defend Britain.

Ron had developed a taste for driving since going back and forth to the North Hangar. He acquired a civilian driving licence, so he could drive otherwise than on duty. Driving tests having been suspended for the duration of the war, his provisional licence was sufficient to drive about privately, if he could get a car. He wrote to his Uncle Don, the farmer whose Humber Chummy he had used as a student. Not only did he still have the little car, but it was not being used and Uncle Don was happy to lend it to his nephew. Uncle Don duly invited Ron down to collect it.

The trip to the farm presented an opportunity for a weekend away and both he and Joan applied for a 72-hour pass. There was no problem getting these granted, but the CO wanted contact details in case anything came up. They travelled down by train, in civvies this time. Uncle Don met them at the railway station with a horse and cart, Don explaining that the horse did not require petrol coupons!

Ron introduced Joan to Don and his Aunty Betty, who made a great fuss of her. Don and Betty ran the farm which had a variety of livestock and a small amount of arable. Don's elderly mother, Ron's great aunt Gertie, also lived on the farm. Although she was reasonably fit for her age, she was a little hard of hearing.

Aunty Gertie was a great character who seemed to be able to see humour at every turn. She made jokes and got other people laughing too. Ron answered as many questions as he could about life in the RAF, but being careful about security. They were impressed that he now had a commission.

Ron and Joan had a great couple of days. Petrol might be rationed, but on the farm, food was more freely available and deliciously fresh. The car was in the barn where it had been for months. Joan helped Ron clean it up, Uncle Don fixed a flat tyre and they started it with the handle as the battery was flat. Joan got very involved with changing the wheel and getting the car going, showing a mechanical aptitude which Ron felt he lacked. They took a trial run to the village pub. Over a pint, they reflected on the life of rural England that they were fighting to protect. Ron knew that Don and his wife had a hard life running the farm, as did everyone in the countryside. There were long hours for farmers and it was hard work looking after animals and crops, but right now it looked like a beautiful idyll away from thoughts of occupied Europe, persecution and war.

Having got the car working, Ron and Joan helped out as much as they could with minor jobs and did some walking in the countryside. The drive back to the base would probably take all day and they did not want any difficulty about being late back and overrunning their pass. Over a stupendous breakfast of bacon and eggs Ron and Joan were debating what time they should leave the next day to get back to Whittingsmoor on time, when they heard the phone ring in the hall. The farm had a phone for emergencies, but was used rarely. His Uncle Don was out in the yard and the phone was answered by his Auntie Gertie. She opened the window and shouted to Uncle Don. “There‘s a man on the phone and he says it’s something about ordering more room and there’s a fault in the left hen coop. Are we doing work on the chicken runs?”

Don could not imagine what his mother was talking about and shouted back. "Tell him to hang on – I'm coming in." Though she was keen to answer the phone - it was something of a novelty – usually his mother could not hear clearly enough to hold a conversation.

Don picked up the phone. "Hello, Holt Farm....yes that's right. Sorry, it's a bad line."

A voice on the other end said, "It's the orderly room at RAF Whittingsmore. Is Flight Lieutenant Cooper there?

"Yes. ... Oh, yes, he's here." Uncle Don put the phone on the hall table. He called through to the kitchen of the rambling farm house. "Ron – it's for you."

Ron shot a glance at Joan and went into the hall. When he had left his uncle said to his mother, "What did you say about the phone call?"

She giggled – a coy laugh that belied her advancing years. "Did I get it wrong then? I thought he said there's a fault in the left hen coop and something about ordering more room."

As Ron returned to the kitchen, Don started to laugh, so it made it difficult to get the words out. He repeated, "A fault in the left hen coop! Flight Lieutenant Cooper is what he said!" He pointed at Ron and grinned. Aunty Gertie became helpless with laughter, which as it always did, infected everyone else. The laughter restarted when they pointed out that an RAF Orderly Room was the administrative centre for a military base.

When they calmed down, Uncle Don said, "Sorry, we should be hoping it's not bad news.".

Ron shook his head. "No, not really." He gave a knowing look to Joan. "An old university friend has been in touch." Joan clapped her hands together, and smiled in an expression of happiness and a little relief. Ron went on. "Some slight bad news though – we'll have to get back for 1400 tomorrow, so we will have to leave early when it gets light."

Uncle Don said, "First light – ha! Come down here again in the winter when we have to get up and break up the ice for the animals well before dawn." He gave Ron a friendly jab in the ribs.

Joan started to clear up the breakfast things. "Well at least we can do the washing up! Come on Ron."

When Ron and Joan were alone at the kitchen sink, she asked about the call. Ron replied, "Not much more than I said, and they were being discreet. Nicholson wants us back for meeting tomorrow, as our university friend has sent us a message."

Joan concluded optimistically. "Wolfgang got back ok then. Maybe the plan is working."

"Let us hope so, but it's easy for things to go wrong. But yes, my guess is that Wolfgang has made it back and is transmitting in code. As we saw a little while ago – you can make all sorts of interpretations of an unclear message."

Joan laughed "Come on you old hen coop, let's finish these dishes!"

*

When the group led by Fleischer and the others failed to return to the barracks near Castel in France, Konrad Nagel sent out men to look for them. Nagel was the Feldwebel – the Wehrmacht equivalent of Sergeant – and the man in charge of the unit where Fleischer and the others were based. Nagel reasoned that it would not take long to find them. After all they were in a fairly large lorry and there were a limited number of towns on the circuit that they were supposed to patrol. He would give them hell when they finally got back. Nagel was in charge of the barracks, while the senior officers were away for a two-day briefing. He wanted it sorted out before the officers returned.

It was general knowledge among the soldiers in the barracks that the patrol was used to requisition supplies – supplies that added to the comfort of the men. The patrol usually consisted of a tour of bars, cafes and restaurants where the occupying soldiers could get what they wanted without too much fear of being reported by any troublesome French hoteliers. Their unit took the view that supplies of best French wine were war booty.

Nearly a whole day had gone by from the time they should have returned and Nagel was getting worried, when he heard one of their motorbikes roar into the yard outside. The rider dashed in and started to give a breathless report. Nagel told him, "Calm down, calm down. Have you found them? Where are they?"

The agitated rider replied "About 5 km southeast of here, but….."

Nagel interrupted, "What are they doing there? How did you find them?"

It was going to be a difficult message to give. The motorcyclist made his report as briefly as he could. "They had been seen leaving a bar just before midnight and all in a drunken state. A gendarme at the end of his shift said he had been nearly knocked off his bike by the lorry which was weaving all over the road. They must have lost their way." He took a deep breath. "But now they are all dead!"

Nagel took a minute to assimilate the words. "Dead? All dead?" Nagel could not believe it. "What in God's name happened to them?"

"Not sure. The truck's parked well off the road down a track, in the middle of nowhere. If the gendarme hadn't seen it passing in that direction it might have taken days to find them. It looks to me that a fight broke out between them. The whole thing smells of drink."

Nagel started to think fast. This was bad news, apart from the obvious loss of his colleagues. HQ would come down on them like a ton of bricks if the messenger was right. "How many people know about this?"

"Just you and me. I just got straight over here as soon as I found them."

"Ok. Go and get Weissmüller. I will get a car, then you will show us the way." Nagel knew that Weissmüller had been a policeman before joining the Wehrmacht. He might be able to help work out what had happened.

Half an hour later the three of them were at the scene of the massacre. It certainly was a mess. Nagel said "What do you think Weissmüller? Could it have been an ambush? The French partisans further south have done some things like this."

Although he had suggested it, this was a conclusion that Nagel didn't want to think about.

Weissmüller looked around. "Didn't you say they were lost and off their usual route? How would the partisans know they were coming? In any case it's not a spot for making an ambush – we are in the middle of an open field."

Only one body was lying on the ground, dead from a knife wound. Next to him was a bayonet covered in dried blood. Of the other three, two were in the back, one leaning over the side and the fourth in the cab. "Apart from Fleischer himself, who has been stabbed, the others look like they've been shot."

Weissmüller went round to the other side of the lorry and opened the cab door on the side where the corpse was lounging against it. Holding the dead man's body to stop it falling, he examined the entry and exit wounds. "This man has been shot through the neck. The shot has come across the cab. It must have been fired from where Fleischer is lying now. Are there any cartridge cases there on the driver's side?"

Nagel looked down, and saw a pistol lying on the ground and several empty cartridge cases. "Yes there are."

Weissmüller looked back at the inside of the door. In the centre of the bloodstain splash there was a bullet buried just below the window in the timber trim. He prised it out and walked back to show Nagel. Nagel removed one of the rounds remaining in the pistol. The bullet from the door was misshapen, but looked like a match. Weissmüller smelt the muzzle.

Weissmüller now examined the soldier hanging over the side of the truck. He did not lift his arm and spot the knife wound, but saw that the man had been shot in the face. "There are burn marks here – this man has been shot at close range." He climbed into the back of the truck stepping over wine bottles that were rolling everywhere. The whole lorry stank of stale wine. The other man's machine gun was still in his hand. Weissmüller peeled back the man's fingers and examined the weapon. "It smells like it's been fired and there are quite a few rounds missing from the magazine." He jumped down and looked at the ground around Fleischer's body. In the soft dry earth he pointed out several small holes. Taking out his own bayonet, he probed the ground and recovered a bullet in remarkably good condition. He repeated the process for a second bullet and handed them to Nagel.

Despite his concern for the situation they were all in, Nagel was impressed by Weissmüller's detective work. Weissmüller took a pencil from his pocket and slid it into the third hole so that it contacted the bullet. It pointed out the angle of entry. "These rounds were fired downwards from the back of the lorry."

Nagel could see from the spent rounds he held in his hand that they were probably their own standard issue, albeit without the cartridge case. He got up on the back of the truck and found spent cartridge cases. Picking up one of the cartridge cases he matched it to the bullets. Nagel said "If it had been an ambush, he would be firing outwards not down over the edge of the side boards, wouldn't he?"

Weissmüller agreed. "With all this evidence, there is no doubt this is all close quarters stuff – I think we can rule out an ambush. The shots were fired from the back of the truck or right by the cab door."

Nagel checked his own conclusion with Weissmüller. "These men have all been killed by the weapons that are here – their own weapons. You agree?"

Weissmüller nodded. "The bodies smell of drink, as does everything." He jerked his thumb over his shoulder in the direction of the motorcycle rider who had found them, who was now keeping a lookout at the gap in a hedgerow where the track left the road. "But I think our friend is right, there must have been a fight between them. They all managed to kill one another in a drunken stupefied rage..."

Nagel leaned on the side of the truck. "Look – only three of us know about this. If we report exactly what we found, all hell will break loose and the whole unit will be in big trouble. We'll all get transferred to shit shovelling or worse. Can we cover it up? We could blame the French Partisans, maybe?"

"That will mean a huge amount of running about and picking up people who know nothing. The SS and Gestapo will be stamping around. Even if they believed the story, I think we would still be in trouble for being careless. And a lot of French people would suffer for no reason"

Nagel could see that would be bad too. He had second thoughts. "And any sort of proper investigation will probably come to the same conclusion as us, in which case we will be back in trouble."

Weissmüller had an alternative. "What about a road accident?"

Nagel was listening. "Ok, try me – how does that work then?"

"There are lots of bomb and shell craters around these parts, from when the English retreated. We passed one at the edge of the road back there. I've brought a camera to record our investigation. We push the truck into the crater, photograph it tipped up at a crazy angle with the bodies on view and say they all got killed in the impact."

"It's worth a try as long as we can keep it quiet. We'll have to bag up the bodies ourselves and get them buried as soon as possible. You don't get bullet wounds in a road accident."

Weissmüller didn't like fiddling evidence, but could see no good could come of higher authorities finding out what they had discovered. Without disguising events, his dead colleagues would be posthumously disgraced and this would reflect on the whole unit. "We had better get on with it. The light won't last much longer if we are going to take photographs."

Chapter 13

Ron and Joan had left the farm early and travelled back to Whittingsmore in the little car that Ron's uncle had loaned him. Rationing of petrol would not be a problem for the small amount of running around locally when they got back, Ron hoped, but he had rather used up the farm's allocation filling the tank and an additional can for the journey. It wasn't the most modern vehicle and not particularly comfortable. But the weather had been kind, and by making an early start they had been able to take frequent stops for elevenses and lunch. When they neared the RAF airfield they drove by a route that brought them straight to the gate on the north side. This would save them going through the main gate and across the airfield to the north hangar for the meeting called by Nicholson and Smith. Ron had not approached the SOE(A) base from this direction before – he always came across the aerodrome, or rather round the perimeter road, but inside the fence. They found the metal gate closed, the gate that Ron had first opened to admit the SOE team all those month ago. Back then, there was no one around and the approach road had been unused for years, but now the gate was manned by guards, housed in a lean-to built on the side of the hangar. As they stopped the car close to the metal mesh, Ron could see that the gate had seen quite a bit of use – the roadway was marked with a fresh scored arc where the gate brushed the road surface. He made a mental note to get that looked at.

A young looking guard sauntered over to them, unslinging his rifle from over his shoulder as he walked. He stood inside the gate cradling the rifle at a diagonal angle in front of his body. He made no move to open the gate. He waited for Ron to get out of the car. When Ron did so, the guard spoke first as he approached. "No entry here mate, turn round right now and clear off."

Ron knew a few of the RAF regiment guards at Whittingsmoor either by sight or because he had spoken with them before, but this one was new, he guessed. "Actually I was hoping you would let us in. I…" Ron didn't finish before being interrupted.

"I won't tell you again, clear off right now."

A second guard was approaching carrying a clipboard. Everyone on an RAF station knew that carrying a clipboard was even better than a slip of paper for walking round for a lot of the day with minimum challenge, as long as you looked purposeful. Whilst it could be a useful ploy for skivers, on this occasion, its use was real. "Who's this then? They're not on the list." He didn't wait for an answer, but turned to Ron. "You've no business here. What do you want?"

Ron didn't know this guard either, and now realised that the orders of the day had not had the names of Joan Newcombe and Ron Cooper added, and these guards had standing orders signed by both himself and Ryland. Those standing orders instructed those persons charged with security not to admit anyone through this gate unless they were on the list. Ron thought 'Ah ha! Hoist with my own petard'. Added to that, neither he nor Joan were in uniform. In a split-second of reflection, Ron wondered if the guard was being overly robust, especially the not-so-subtle brandishment of his rifle, or was the guard just accurately following Ron's own orders? He then noticed that the first guard's attention was focused over his shoulder and Ron quickly became aware of Joan's presence to his left.

"Hello darling, we would probably let you in", the guard leered at Joan, who immediately produced her RAF identity card.

"Don't be a B. F. Private", she snapped, and as she profferred the card, asserted "Section Officer Newcombe…."

"And Flight Lieutenant Cooper" interrupted Ron, producing his own ID card. "Now get that gate open. It was me that signed your orders." Ron was now irked by the guard's attitude.

The other guard seemed to have a bit more idea of decorum – he was a corporal Ron noticed, and this one was quick with a face saver. "Yes Sir, Ma'am, but I'll need you to countersign an amendment." He gestured to the other guard to open the gate and flicked through papers on the clipboard.

The first guard somewhat sullenly said, "You're sure this is all right?"

"Just get on with it", snapped Ron. "I'll give the Corporal his written order."

"Ok, ok", grunted the guard and moved to open the gate, although he didn't rush himself.

Joan said, "If that gate is not open in five seconds you'll be on a charge." And she marched back to the car exuding an expectation that her order would be obeyed without question.

Ron made an alteration to the written orders on the clipboard. *'Admit F/L Cooper and S/O Newcombe'* and signed it. To the relief of the Corporal, the signature matched perfectly to one already on the order in his possession. Mind you, he found that the writing and the signatures were almost unreadable squiggles. The corporal thought to himself, 'Might be an officer, but can't write his own name', but wisely kept those thoughts to himself. His colleague had already upset the officers quite enough for one day.

Ron gave the guards a short lecture. “You can keep the gates secure and still be civil.” The guards now looked flushed and uncomfortable. He turned to the Private. “And the correct response to an order from an officer is not an ok, ok….but Yes Sir or Yes Ma’am.” Ron spun on his heel, returned to the car and drove through the gate. Neither he nor Joan looked at the guards as they passed through, but as they approached the hangar building they exchanged amused glances at one another once out of sight of the guards.

Ron made an aside to Joan as he made a crashing noise with the gears. “Hum…. Don’t be a B. F. is not a very ladylike expression!”

Joan tossed her hair the way she did when she was pleased with herself. “It worked didn’t it?”

As they turned around the corner of the hangar and approached the main doors, they saw Frank Nash and a couple of other SOE men drinking tea and having a smoke just outside. Ron pulled up next to them.

Frank greeted them “Hello Coop old boy, hello miss.” I see you’ve got past our new guards. ” He winked and waved them into the hangar.

Ron parked up inside the hangar, which he noticed had more unidentified vehicles and unspecified objects covered up with sheets every time he came in. They walked into the office and found Nicholson alone. He informed them that Smith was on his way and expected at any time. Ron and Joan took turns visiting the toilet – bumping along potholed roads all day in the tiny car did have an effect on the bladder. By the time they had made a cup of tea, Smith had arrived. He dropped his bag on the desk. “I see you have smartened up the guards on the gate. They were both standing to attention when they checked me in.” Neither

Ron nor Joan said anything, but noted to themselves that their interaction with the guards had achieved some effect.

They soon got down to the business of the meeting. Smith pulled some papers from his briefcase. They were typed transcripts of messages on flimsy paper. "Now then, we have received these messages purporting to come from Cooper's man Schultze. Unfortunately, our people have hung onto them for quite a while, not realising our interest in them. It has lost us some time. I say purporting, because we have developed an extra degree of caution since the news that our agents had been compromised, news that you brought us Ron. We want to be sure that this communication is from a sound source. Your source Ron... " he gestured towards Ron and Joan " ... it is only you two that have met this chap. We want your opinion about any doubts of authenticity as we go along. Understood?"

Joan asked, "Is there anything to make us think it's not right?"

Smith blew out his cheeks. "Not really – in fact the job today is to work out the content of the messages, which is what I propose we do next."

Ron said, "We will have to see what's in the messages first, I suppose, before we can get any clue about authenticity – if we can decipher them, that is."

Smith turned the papers round on the desk so that Ron could read them.

Ron fingered the sheets of paper. "If it's Wolfgang, I am expecting an apparently random set of letters and numbers that we can arrange in groups of four."

"That applies to the messages that we normally intercept, I'm afraid. Our code breakers have had a go at these already and couldn't make anything of them, using their… "Smith shot a glance at Joan "… using our usual methods. You'll forgive me miss, if I don't go into that."

Joan was well aware of the clandestine nature of Smith's world and knew that she was only on the edge of a web of secrets. She responded, "Of course."

Ron continued his perusal of the papers. "No, he won't be encoding them in the usual way – he will want them to look random both to us and to his own side. I agreed a structure with him based on prime numbers. If we find any meaning it will be locked up in the groups corresponding to prime numbers." Ron picked up a foolscap note pad.

Nicholson asked, "So, can we work them out? Surely the idea is to show us the places and dates where we can find Hartmann? We can't even make guesses about where Hartmann's team might be – they're in a train after all. We can't just fly photo recon all over Germany looking for them."

Ron was in his element. It would be like a University tutorial and this bit felt like a game to him. Maybe the stuff that Smith and Nicholson got up to felt like a game to them. Ron laid out the sheet of intercepts, which had already been arranged in four character groups:

N578	FE14	12XM	DFZH	09AP	NGHS	M11X	RT6L
CG6M	45FG	GIZP	FG5N	NEHC	ABER	56GH	ZB5H
XGRU	56B0	GRUB	GHTR	GF5H	BNYF	IELX	56NG
GELM	DFTN	45G6	NAN7	NEUM	THNO	ASBO	RT56
THRC	4NGJ	NGHT	COAN	MAHX	67NA	NHT3	BHRL
RTSX	KLNT						

Ron wrote numbers over each group. "Let's number the groups."

1	2	3	4	5	6	7	8
N578	FE14	12XM	DFZH	09AP	NGHS	M11X	RT6L
9	10	11	12	13	14	15	16
CG6M	45FG	GIZP	FG5N	NEHC	ABER	56GH	ZB5H
17	18	19	20	21	22	23	24
XGRU	56B0	GRUB	GHTR	GF5H	BNYF	IELX	56NG
25	26	27	28	29	30	31	32
GELM	DFTN	45G6	NAN7	NEUM	THNO	ASBO	RT56
33	34	35	36	37	38	39	40
THRC	4NGJ	NGHT	COAN	MAHX	67NA	NHT3	BHRL
41	42						
RTSX	KLNT						

Ron continued, while the others listened without comment. "Now then, the significant stuff should be in the groups we can find from the prime numbers. He wrote these down on the pad. 2, 3, 5, 7, 11, 13, 17, 19, 23, 29, 31, 37, 41. "A prime number is one that can only be divided by itself and one. So let's look at the primes." He heavily over-wrote the characters of the groups corresponding to the numbers on his pad.

1	2	3	4	5	6	7	8
N578	**FE14**	**12XM**	DFZH	**09AP**	NGHS	**M11X**	RT6L
9	10	11	12	13	14	15	16
CG6M	45FG	**GIZP**	FG5N	**NEHC**	ABER	56GH	ZB5H
17	18	19	20	21	22	23	24
XGRU	56B0	**GRUB**	GHTR	GF5H	BNYF	**IELX**	56NG
25	26	27	28	29	30	31	32
GELM	DFTN	45G6	NAN7	**NEUM**	THNO	**ASBO**	RT56
33	34	35	36	37	38	39	40
THRC	4NGJ	NGHT	COAN	**MAHX**	67NA	NHT3	BHRL
41	42						
RTSX	KLNT						

Nicholson got up to stand behind Ron and look over his shoulder. The other two sat each side as Ron pointed out groups with his pencil. “I would say if there is a number in the group, it’s probably a date and if just characters it would be a place – a town. If so, the first few prime numbers tell us where to look for dates – that’s the second, third, fifth and seventh groups. The eleventh group looks more like a place, so it seems we have four dates.” Ron wrote the groups down on a separate sheet. He immediately added a date.

FE14	
12XM	
09AP	9 April
M11X	

“So FE14, 12XM, then 09AP that one must be ninth of April. Then lastly M11X.”

“The first one would be February fourteenth.” Ron wrote it in.

FE14	Feb 14
12XM	
09AP	9 April
M11X	

Smith interjected “We know the Germans tend to use an X as blank character. So the other two would be March and May respectively – if they are in chronological order.”

“Yes – I think so.” Ron overwrote the key characters leaving the X characters feint, which he then rubbed out with an eraser.

FE14	Feb 14
12XM	12 March
09AP	9 April
M11X	11 May

Nicholson was already imagining an operation, wondering about timing and planning. “If this is right, some of the dates have passed, so we are already a bit late. We are going to have a rush to get an op going.”

Smith thought it looked plausible. “Although he is using a different format to disguise each group, presumably to avoid discovery at his end if anyone checks, I would say its the real thing if Ron is reading the encoding correctly. Pity about the delay though, but I’m sure you’ll work out something Nicholson, you usually do.”

Joan commented. “So the X is a blank and the order shuffled about as a disguise. He’s being careful about discovery. More careful than the girls he talks to in Swedish bars!”

“Do you mean that is out of character?” Smith was checking.

Joan clarified. “I wasn’t being entirely serious, but no. Once he knew who we were he did become very careful.”

“Now then,” said Ron, “The towns that the dates would apply to, we can expect to find secreted in groups eleven, thirteen, seventeen and nineteen. They are the next primes.” He wrote these next groups down opposite dates.

FE14	Feb 14	GIZP
12XM	12 March	NEHC
09AP	9 April	XGRU
M11X	11 May	GRUB

Ron continued to assemble the table of dates with corresponding letters. “Let’s have a look at the next prime numbered groups. That’s groups 23, 29, 31 and 37.”

FE14	Feb 14	GIZP	IELX
12XM	12 March	NEHC	NEUM
09AP	9 April	XGRU	BSSA
M11X	11 May	GRUB	MAHX

"And the prime number after that is 41. Hum – that's a bit of an orphan. Where might that fit in I wonder?"

Ron erased the X characters and wrote the 'orphan' group at the end.

FE14	Feb 14	GIZP	IELX
12XM	12 March	NEHC	NEUM
09AP	9 April	XGRU	BSSA
M11X	11 May	GRUB	MAHX

RTSX

For a few moments they stared blankly at the paper. Nicholson said "They don't look like any names I recognise. Maybe we are decoding wrongly, or the message is actually random."

A few more seconds passed with the group keeping thoughtful silence, then Joan jumped a little. She had had a 'eureka' moment. Joan picked up a pencil and wrote on another sheet. "It's reversed!"

LEI PZIG
MUEN CHEN
ASSB URG
HAMB URG

Now the names leapt of the page at them: Leipzig, Munich – spelt in the German way – and Hamburg.

Smith was ecstatic. "Brilliant. Well done Joan – how could you see that?"

"I do crosswords and word games. Spelling stuff backwards often crops up."

Ron finished the job. "Ah, so that's how the last group of letters is used. A town with a name too big for two eight character groups, so he's just added it on." Ron added the last group to the third line and rewrote the last column backwards.

FE14	Feb 14	GIZP	IELX		- XLEIPZIG
12XM	12 March	NEHC	NEUM		- MUENCHEN
09AP	9 April	XGRU	BSSA	RTSX	- XSTRASSBURGX
M11X	11 May	GRUB	MAHX		- HAMBURGX

Nicholson now saw his target list. "Well done Joan and to you Ron – and I suppose to Schultze, for thinking up such a fiendish code – and working out that you would be able to crack it, Ron."

"His last words to me were, 'Look for the primes'. If you know the letters are in groups of four….. well we did it anyway." Ron looked thoughtfully at the list they had unravelled from the brain of a man on the other side of Europe, through the common thread of a mathematical device. Was it plausible and genuine? He thought out loud. "Leipzig, Munich, Strasbourg and Hamburg. I think these are all places with Universities, so it makes sense for them to go there."

Smith wanted to finally reassure himself that there was no falsehood in the message. "This looks genuine to me. It is telling us that the coding team are in a train which is presently located in Munich, shortly to be moved to Strasbourg, where it will remain for a month or so. There could be no advantage for the Germans in feeding us information like that, could there? Are we agreed that this is a suitable basis for planning and these messages do indeed come from Schultze?"

They all nodded and Nicholson noted the agreement from the others. "Ok – let's go for it. They are all big towns, so finding the train is not that simple – especially since we don't really have any effective network of agents in Germany."

Smith pointed at the third line of the table, tapping gently on the desk through the paper. "The Strasbourg one is interesting. The

Germans might think it's in Germany, but the French have other ideas. I see that it is spelt the German way here."

Nicholson said "Looks like the best of the bunch."

Smith responded. "Yes. I think we have a report on the area saying the population are pretty fed up with the usual Nazi behaviour in occupation. We would be able to get agents in there better than the rest."

"We are talking of an air strike here I presume, as on the château." Ron was thinking how his RAF colleagues could mount such an attack. "It's closer than the German cities as well, isn't it? Have you got a map?"

While Ron looked at a map, Nicholson produced a couple of personnel files. "We need to talk about the Welsh-speaking ground controller."

Joan picked up the files and flicked through them. "Evans and Woodward have practiced on the bombing range with the three best men we chose. We code named them Lion, Tiger and Falcon. Lion is – as we know – dead. Falcon looks the better bet of the other two. He was a school teacher, has studied in Alsace-Lorraine and speaks fluent French and German – as well as Welsh and English."Nicholson had reviewed all the candidates and reminded himself about them by looking at the file. "Yes you're right. He's not the action man type that Lion was, but we want someone that can merge into the population of the city. With a bit of luck he can help quite a bit with reconnoitring that target. We will want to make sure Hartmann is there. We can supply Falcon with photos of Hartmann and Schultze from old university records we have found."

Smith said, "We must make sure that the aircrew know as little as possible about Falcon, and why they are attacking this train.

The whole thing must be like a normal raid. If they get shot down and captured, the less they know the better."

Chapter 14

Ron got an appointment with Ryland as soon as he could, which was the next morning. He needed to do his 'liaison bit' with Bomber Command ops. For a full scale raid, which was what was required to disguise their purpose, Ryland would have to issue the orders.

Ryland was as businesslike as ever, but Ron thought he looked a little tired. "SOE are looking to repeat the type of operation we did in Belgium, Sir. But there will be a number of differences."

"Ok. What do you need?"

"It will be a precision attack from our special Mosquito, followed up by an obliteration job, to cover our tracks. The more it looks like a normal bomber mission, the better. The target will be a railway yard in Strasbourg on the German French border. A bit further than last time."

Ryland was somewhat acerbic. "I trust we are not talking about a daylight raid – that is out of the question for that distance."

"No, I was expecting we have to do the job at night. Apart from the danger of flying during daytime, it would look abnormal. The first wave – the precision attack – wants to be followed up by a full scale raid by our heavies. That first wave would involve the special Mosquito and three or four light bombers, also Mosquitoes in the plan, with a bomb load."

"We do just that with our new pathfinder tactics. The Mosquitoes hit first with flares and incendiaries and the main force bomb on that. The pathfinders have to be accurate of course." Ryland added, "It would look normal to everyone on our side – and to the enemy."

"Yes Sir. I have also come to the conclusion that Whisky Sugar – the souped-up turret-less Lancaster – won't be fast enough to work things the way we did on the Belgian job. It nearly got caught then and it won't do this time. But, say, three accompanying Mosquitoes could carry a good bomb load and support the first phase, prior to the main force. I am going to see Squadron Leader Askew and tell him he was right about the turret-less Lancaster on this sort of job. He wasn't convinced, as you know Sir. It was my idea and it should come from me Sir, if you don't mind."

Ryland sighed, got up and walked to the window, his back to Ron, who had seen Ryland look into space before when thinking things through. There was a drizzle of rain outside. Ryland watched the rivulets of water run erratically down the pane."That won't be possible, Cooper. Askew was killed last night. His aircraft was caught by a night fighter, we think. It was seen to blow up in mid air – no survivors."

Everyone knew the odds were against the crews who went out over occupied Europe night after night. Much of the time one could try to see the losses as just names and numbers, but they were real people – friends and acquaintances. Ryland would have relied on Askew more than most of the other officers. There was a brief silence.

"The level of losses has increased a bit lately. We're losing too many good men, but we've got to be in it for the long haul." He drew his breath in, an expression of resolve, and turned back to Ron. "If you want a full-scale raid you can have one. You know you have support right from the top. When do you want this to be?"

"Between 9th April and 11th May."

"Crumbs! That's very precise. And soon."

"Ah, although that's the window of time when our target will be in Strasbourg – we have to do some planning, so can't fix a date yet. My guess will be towards the end of the period."

"Ok – you let me know as soon as you can about dates." Ryland termninated the meeting. "Now, I've got some letters to write."

*

Ron called Woodward and Evans to a meeting in the North hangar. Ron found them looking round the special Mosquito, with Woodward strolling round the modified machine and patting it in an affectionate sort of way. It was somehow a reassuring sight.

Ron walked over and met them under the shadow of the aeroplane. Although much smaller than a big four-engined bomber like a Stirling or a Lancaster, it still towered above them. The two crewmen saluted as he approached.

"Morning chaps." Ron got straight on with an update. "The next mission for you two will be a bit trickier than the last one. The target will be about twice as far, and you will have to do it under cover of darkness. The target is smaller as well. It's a train. You have to shoot it up the way you did before. The only good news is that the train will not be moving."

Woodward produced a half smile. "Not moving – well that's something. But this does sound difficult. You know how we have trouble hitting targets accurately at night on normal raids. Where will the train be?"

"We're not sure yet, probably in a siding. We are planning to wait for a night with a good moon, and we are going to use the Oboe radio navigation again. That was pretty accurate the last time."

Rhys Evans asked, "Will we be talked in again the way we were before? By the Welsh guy Lion observing and giving us target information, I mean?"

Evans was unaware of the fate of Lion. There was no need for him to know the man was dead. In fact the two Welshmen had never met – only talked over the radio, plus that initial 'interview test' over the phone in London. During the rehearsals over the practice bombing site, Lion and the other Welsh speaking observers with whom they had trained had been based in Scotland. There, they awaited the Mosquito on its flight from Whittingsmore to come and pound the target with the heavy cannon mounted in the nose of the aircraft. The training missions attempted to simulate what would happen on the raid – coming into radio range with difficult reception, then talking in the attack, using Welsh. All in the shortest possible time to avoid detection by direction-finding radio equipment. It was presumed the enemy would be listening in during the attack. Ron resumed. "It will be a different observer, but yes, there will be a Welsh-speaking agent talking you into the target. It will be one of the three you have practised with – Falcon probably." Woodward and Evans only knew the ground controllers by their code names. " It worked all right the last time didn't it?"

"Well, yes and no." Evans explained. "We line up the target by shooting tracer. The agent on the ground told us if we were shooting in the right place before we let fly with the cannon. It's all very well, but there's a hell of a lot happening in a short space of time. What with the noise of the guns firing the tracer as well as the noise in the Mossie, it's quite difficult to hear."

Ron could see the problem, although he had not experienced an attack himself. But he did know how noisy it was in a Mosquito in flight, even without all the shooting.

Ron's appreciation of the difficulty of the task added to his awkward feelings in sending people out to do a job for which he had no experience or talent himself. And it wasn't just Ron. Privately, Nicholson and the SOE boys had been concerned beforehand about the low chances of success for the Belgian raid and felt they were lucky it had gone so well. Ron tried to empathise with the aircrew. "I can imagine this is a bit demanding. We'll have to think of something."

Evans said, "I have."

"What?" Apparently this came as a surprise to Woodward.

"I've got an idea about lining up a shot for the cannon."

Woodward said, "Let's hear it. We've had lots of ideas for this project – another one won't hurt."

Evans walked round and pointed to the muzzle of the cannon. "When I was in the hills, and using a smaller gun to this one, we used to shoot rabbits and foxes sometimes. We used to tie a torch to the barrel. Where the torch lit up was where the shot would go."

Woodward wondered quite what Evans had in mind. "So we tie a torch to our Molins cannon?"

Evans continued. "Not exactly, but same idea. Could we put a searchlight on the Mossie to give a ….what's the English word light .. narrow…"

Ron interjected, "Beam – you mean a beam – to point where we're going to shoot."

"Yes. My idea is a beam of light as an aiming guide instead of using our tracer guns."

Woodward was prepared to listen, but it sounded daft. "Surely we'd be a sitting duck. Jerry will just shoot at the light. And that means shooting at us!"

Evans had thought of that. "I also suggest to shine it down a tube – something a few feet long."

Evans and Ron watched as Woodward walked to the front of the aeroplane and stared at it thoughtfully from dead ahead. "Ah, I see. So this tube will constrain the light to a beam and you would only be able to see it from dead ahead." He was warming to the task. "I suppose we would only turn it on just before opening fire. Okay, I can see the theory, but where on earth would we mount it? I wonder how much space and weight something like that requires. We are going to have to do something, or we stand no chance of hitting a small target in the dark. What do you think Sir?"

"I'll talk to Nash and Sykes and if it looks like a goer we can meet in the North Hangar at ten hundred tomorrow. Oh, one other thing. We think that the target train will be in the town with a river running through it. So you should be able to pick out some landmarks in the moonlight. With the river, the railways and Oboe we hope it will be enough to find the train."

*

That evening, Ron made a date with Joan. He arranged for a four hour pass and went over to Joan's cottage. They enjoyed a meal together, some of the ingredients of which used up the last of the supplies brought back in a small hamper from the farm trip. It supplemented the somewhat meagre allocation confined by the limits of the ration book. Ron thought they might go to the local pub afterwards, but the 'careless talk cost lives' campaign hit home and they stayed in. He wanted to talk through some of the things on his mind. You wouldn't want to do that in the pub.

As they cleared up after the meal, Ron approached the subject that had been in his thoughts. He was wrestling with his conscience on two matters, both of which he found awkward and humbling. "You know Askew has been killed on a raid?"

"I heard." They both knew Askew and some of the others in his crew.

"You've worked out, I suppose, that this job we're on is going to result in an attack on a target. The target that Wolfgang's messages identified."

"Of course. It's pretty obvious that something will be done with the information, and all the Welsh-speakers that are tied up with it – but I'm not going to ask about any details. These are the rules of the game aren't they?"

"Yup, they are. But not many people know about how the attack might be put together and SOE don't want to expand the circle of knowledge. So it's fallen to me, now that Askew has been lost, to end up telling the crew how they might mount an attack. Me, a non-operational backroom-boy telling these guys how to do the job I couldn't do myself. Even being in an aeroplane makes me sick."

"I know." Joan smiled. They both remembered that trip in the Mosquito back from Sweden.

They finished drying the dishes and walked back to the fire side in the little sitting-room. Ron put another log on the fire. A slight spring chill had returned to the evenings, and he watched the sparks that rose from the disturbed embers. “It doesn’t seem right. What’s worse is that it is my plan and ideas that led up to all this. Now I am sending aircrew out on a very risky job, while I stay at home.”

“Weren’t you sending them out before?”

“How do you mean?”

“You and I are part of a team – the whole of the RAF and the whole of the country are in it together. Even when you were just getting supplies for the aerodrome, you were helping to send them out. It’s no different now.”

Ron poked the fire. “I suppose I feel uncomfortable – they are risking their lives on my plan and I’m not.”

“When we went over to Sweden – was that a bit risky? You know it was – you realised when we were there.”

Joan had a point and her perspective helped assuage Ron’s concerns. Perhaps his own self-implied and self-directed criticism was misplaced. He had been beginning to see himself like a First World War general sitting behind the lines and leading from the back, rather than leading from the front. Joan’s analysis lifted his mood. He moved on to another aspect that had been bothering him. “What do you make of Wolfgang? He has told us where the coding team will be, a team that he’s part of. He knows we will target it.”

“So he has put himself in harm’s way?”

Ron shuffled in his chair. “Yes – and it has been bothering me. Wolfgang gave us all that information and basically he has put himself right in the firing line, which is not much reward for the help he gave us."

Joan could easily see what he meant. She knew all the players as well. She said, "It's difficult when you know the people who are putting their lives at risk. Usually they're people on our side, British people I mean. When you know someone on the other side it brings it home that we're all human, doesn't it?"

"Yes."

She went on, "Look, surely Wolfgang knew what he was doing when he gave us the information. I guess he's worked out the consequences." She paused. "Given that there will be an attack – and I've worked that out – can't we warn him to stay away when it happens?"

"I tried to think how that might be done. It's out of the question for all sorts of reasons."

"Yes, I suppose we cannot be completely sure that the messages are on the level and from Wolfgang Schultze can we? He might have been found out."

"That's one problem, but there are others. We don't know ourselves when the attack will be – actually we don't even know if it's feasible. There is the weather and all sorts of technical considerations. Even if we did, it's one-way communication. Wolfgang has sent us a message but we have no way of replying. I have tried to think of a way of getting a message to him, even if Nicholson and Smith were to allow it, which of course they won't."

Joan put her arm around Ron and kissed his neck. "Wolfgang's decision was his, not yours. When we were out in Sweden you gave him the option of getting out and coming back with us. He chose this path." She went on, "Has it occurred to you that he might not want to get out of the way? If you save him in some way it might be the worse for his family, the few that are left. If he gets killed by enemy action, well…."

Joan was right again. It didn't stop Ron being uncomfortable with the whole situation, the people he knew and respected being put in danger, but the discussion with Joan had helped him tremendously. Ron was briefly tempted to suggest staying at the cottage overnight, but decided to return to his own billet at the base, getting back before he overran the time on his pass.

At the doorway as they said goodnight, Joan left Ron a final thought. "I was talking to a young Army officer a few months ago. He had been out in Dunkirk. He said something that stuck with me. He said that you can only ask people to risk their necks if it's in a worthy cause – the right cause. And you can only ask them to do that if you're prepared to take risks yourself. He said it's as simple as that. You took those risks, ones you're equipped to take, when you went to Sweden – and we definitely know it's the right cause don't we?"

As Ron wiped the condensation from the windows of his car and headed back, he could see how Joan had got the job dealing with personnel. She was some girl.

Chapter 15

Since the revelation of the dates and locations of the German coding team, there had been an intense period of activity. Rhys Evans's idea to create a narrow pencil beam, to line up the main gun of the special Mosquito, was taken up with enthusiasm by the SOE(A) team. Nicholson and Frank Nash – the SOE(A) 'gadget man' – had discovered that an aircraft-mounted light was already in existence. Called the Leigh light after its inventor – an RAF Officer involved with attacks at sea – it was being used to illuminate target U-Boats from aircraft.

Although it was now known that an airborne light was in service for a very similar tactic, the North Team had some special problems to solve. After some discussion, the Leigh light itself was mounted at the rear end of the Mosquito's bomb bay facing forward, projecting its beam down a tube that ran the length of the bomb doors. It had to be retractable to avoid a drag effect that would slow the aeroplane and negate the main advantage of the Mosquito – the speed. There was the extra weight of batteries to power the light as well, all of which meant that this Mosquito could carry no bombs.

Frank Nash and Bill Sykes, Whittingsmore's maintenance supremo, had worked on the job – demanding a constant stream of parts that challenged Ron's 'Mr Fixit' reputation for getting supplies.

In the attack, the special Mosquito would line up the target using the beam as a sighting aid. The gunner would then direct accurate shell fire from the heavy cannon onto the train, and if possible the coach occupied by key code breaker personnel – notably Hartmann.

The accompanying Mosquitoes would immediately bomb the train and act as a marker for a following mass of over a hundred four-engined bombers. The raid would appear to be a general RAF attack on a railway yard, not at all uncommon.

Evans and Woodward resumed their practice and preparation, this time for a night attack. There had been a delay while their aeroplane was modified. They had spent this time practising, identifying trains in marshalling yards and sidings, using another Mosquito. The idea was to work out what sort of moonlight and weather conditions would make an attack possible, but "Bloody impossible!" was Woodward's judgement.

Not only was it a frighteningly difficult task locating a specific train in the practice runs, but flying about over Britain's towns brought another problem. Often they encountered firing from the air defences, who unsurprisingly thought they were under enemy attack. After a couple of near-misses it was decided to abort training runs until the converted special Mosquito was ready.

Meanwhile, SOE(A) had organised some reconnaissance photographic sorties over Strasbourg. Ron and Nicholson called a briefing meeting with Evans and Woodward to try and resolve the location issue.

Just before the aircrew arrived Nicholson updated Ron. "Your man Schultze has been pretty accurate so far. We have looked for the train with photo reconnaissance in the locations he told us."

"So we've not much idea what this train looks like?"

"We know what it looked like from ground level when it was the Kaiser's train – we have old news photos." He held up a large envelope. "It looks quite different from ordinary trains. It's old, but can be seen to be quite plush accommodation for very important people. But that's not the same as identifying it from the air. Not until yesterday. Our agents have found it now and we have picked it out on the aerial photos. It seems to have arrived in Strasbourg exactly as your man said it would. It's parked on the edge of a railway marshalling yard next to a road. Ah, here are the boys."

They paused as Woodward and Evans joined them. Ron asked, "How's it going chaps?"

"We are going to be lucky to find the target." Said Woodward. Even assuming the Oboe navigation system gets us within sight of the target, which it might not – it's right on the limit at that distance – but at night and unless conditions are perfect we are going to be pretty much stuck to find and single out a specific train."

Ron chipped in, "We know that Oboe is a bit uncertain at that distance, but don't forget you'll be accompanied by the other Mosquitoes, some of which will have a H2S box." H2S was another navigation aid that effectively scanned the ground and worked well when there were coastlines or rivers that could be tied up with a map of the area. As there were identifiable bends in the river through Strasbourg, this was a promising tool for the mission.

Evans was keen to see his idea implemented. "We will just have to fly a circuit or two over the target using the light to find the right train. We haven't tried it out with the light yet."

"The more we fly about, and spend time over the target, the less surprise and more chance of being hit." Woodward was the experienced man and of course was right.

Nicholson gave them the update. “I can give you some news. Three days ago we had a message from the resistance confirming that the train is indeed in Strasbourg and parked in a siding. We flew a recon and were lucky enough to find it on this photograph.” Nicholson produced a large glossy photograph of a town showing a lot of railway yards and a river curving past them. He pointed with a pencil to the bottom left corner of the picture. “It’s only just in, actually half of it is out of shot.”

They all peered at the corner of the photograph. There were three coaches in a siding and a fourth cut off by the edge of the photographic print. It also looked like there were a couple of vehicles parked next to the train with access to the streets of the town. Nicholson continued. “So we know where it is and assuming they don’t move it about, we’ve got our target pinned down.” He produced a street map. “This is a map made before the war and we can see the arrangements of roads and streets near where the train is parked. I have transposed the position from the recon photograph on to this map,” he said, pointing out a pencilled cross at the edge of the railway yard.

Woodward responded. “Don’t suppose there’s any chance of asking the resistance to position men at four or five points down this road and be ready to show a light upwards?” He drew a line down a road that aligned directly with the cross. If it works it would be like an arrow pointing at the target. A bit risky for the chaps doing it though?”

Nicholson shook his head. “No chance I’m afraid. We don’t have that many men and they would just be noticed. No, you will be relying on navigation aids, moonlight and on the ground observer Falcon to talk you in. Sorry.”

*

The man codenamed Falcon and a French patriot watched the dark countryside of rural and somewhat mountainous France roll past under the open bomb-bay doors of the huge Stirling aeroplane. The aircrew referred to them as 'Joes' – the name that had become a convention for the mysterious passengers who they occasionally ferried into occupied Europe. The bomber crew risking their lives every time they took off and crossed the coast had a respectful view of the 'Joes' dropping into enemy occupied territory – it was a different sort of bravery. They talked about these agents of the secret service amongst themselves, but they knew better than to enquire about anything of the passengers themselves. On the way back they were to drop propaganda leaflets over Metz and Nancy, but the mission controllers had made it clear to the skipper that his top priority was get his two Joes on target in the area of eastern France close to the German border near Strasbourg.

Not much could be seen on this slightly cloudy and almost moonless night. Clouds intermittently obscured their view of the ground. So far they had been unmolested by the defending forces, only seeing some misdirected flack earlier in the flight. It was cold inside the fuselage as the wind whipped about the interior. The navigator was confident that they were coming up on the drop zone and all eyes in the aircraft began searching for a light from the waiting Maquis on the ground. The bomb-aimer was the first to spot the signal – not quite dead ahead, but impressive navigation nonetheless. Moments later, the two men were despatched silently out of the aircraft and disappeared from sight below and behind their slipstream. The bomber crew always wondered about the fate of the Joes, but their thoughts quickly turned to ensuring their own safety and fulfilling the mission, before getting safely home.

*

As soon as the Leigh light conversion work was complete, Woodward and Evans set about trying out the alignment and aiming of the cannon. It took a few days to iron out some defects in the retraction mechanism which did not always lower the whole installation accurately – meaning the shots went off target. By the time the engineering team had added a few extra tweaks the thing came into perfect alignment every time. Both Sykes and Nash were pleased to find that they had satisfied customers in Evans and Woodward, especially Evans who had thought of the idea. They continued to practice with the ground controller 'Tiger' talking them in to shoot up various dummy targets on the Scottish bombing range at night. Whilst superior to the alignment method previously employed by using tracer in the machine guns, Woodward was still concerned the light would mark them out as a sitting duck.

*

It was late, well after midnight. Hartmann was entertaining in his plush train in a manner that would have fitted even its former royal user. The catering staff were waiting to clear up the dining car, but the occupants were evidently still having a good time and well into the cigars and brandy. When Hartmann stayed up, everyone else did, including Schultze and the soldier that was one of the radio operators.

"Who's in there this time?" asked the soldier, as he moved a chessman on the board that shared a desk with radio equipment. They had been playing chess to while away the time. The games had been largely one-sided.

"I know the University people but there are also a couple of SS officers. I don't know them. Check mate, by the way."

"That's three times in a row you have beaten me." The radio operator idly checked the wireless set, twiddling the tuning and the volume. Between the hiss and crackle of the static a voice could be heard coming from the headphones lying on the desk. "*Hebog. Hebog. Galwed.*"

"What is that do you think?"

Schultze listened, but the voice was gone, the headphones only making a whistling and hissing as the dial was moved about.

There was a commotion from the corridor. "Sounds like they are leaving." The guests staggered noisily down the corridor and flung open the door of the train. The waiting cars were bathed in light from the open doorway. The guests and Hartmann staggered down the wooden steps provided to permit access to a flat gravelled area at the edge of the railway yard. Tonight three cars were parked there. The drivers, some of whom had been asleep, got out and opened doors for their more senior passengers and tried to look alert.

Schultze lifted the blackout blind to make a gap the width of his hand and peered out. He could see the protracted farewell process. There was much back-slapping and laughter. Hartmann waved them off and turned back towards the train.

Schultze let the blind drop back into place. The radio man was still working the set, thinking about the unintelligible voice. "I heard that same stuff before, about 20 minutes ago. It seems to be one end of a transmission. What language was it?"

Schultze said, "I don't know, I only just caught it. Could it be either Bulgarian or Rumanian?

There were banks of radio equipment in the radio room of the train. Another radio, one tuned to the air defence network, crackled into life. This time the voice was clear and in German. The radio operator picked up another set of headphones and relayed the content to Schultze. "Sounds like the British are making another raid. They are tracking some heavy bombers. Looks like Stuttgart will be getting it again."

"Where was that message from?" Schultze asked.

"I think it came from Rheims. The bombers usually pass through their radar control space. Perhaps we'll see our night fighters catch them this time."

At that moment the first radio broke into life again, much louder than before, as the operator had left the volume turned up. There were definitely sentences in some foreign tongue and it did sound like one end of a conversation. The word 'Hebog' cropped up several times, but as for the rest – it just could not be made out.

Schultze had been expecting something out of the ordinary for weeks. Could this be it? It was a long time since meeting Ron and the British girl in Sweden. He was beginning to think that his elaborately coded messages had not been picked up or understood.

He asked the radio man, "Where's that map?"

The radio operator tossed over a map of southwest France. Schultze ran his finger over a possible route to Strasbourg from Britain. It could be an attack on Stuttgart; the RAF used indirect dog-leg routes to attempt to confuse the defenders about where the targets might be. But just possibly they could be coming to Strasbourg, for an attack on the train – the attack he had been expecting that had not so far materialised. He said, "I'm just going outside."

*

Agent Falcon and the resistance man, known only as Antoine, had made a successful landfall from the parachute drop and linked up with a small resistance group, who had helped them to get to the city of Strasbourg. Time was of the essence in finding the train and confirming who was there. Using his language skills, Falcon had managed to move freely about and had established a surveillance point where he could see the comings and going from the train. Using the old photographs SOE had provided, he had confirmed the presence of Schultze and Hartmann. The intelligence was indeed correct. The raid was on.

Falcon's own radio which he had brought with him was only a short-range set for talking in the attack. Communication with the SOE planners relied on morse code, through the existing network of the French resistance. Falcon coded short messages in Welsh and passed them to the Resistance to send. The message conveyed the information that the targets were here, but the next day he had to recind it and abort any attack as Hartmann disappeared for a day. It was going to be tricky to ensure Hartmann was in situ. But then – a stroke of luck. Catering supplies were being seen delivered to the train. The Resistance soon were able to discover from the caterer that a slap-up party was being planned, with Hartmann as the host. Falcon sent a short message. Now they just needed the weather to be clear.

Night fell. A clear night. There had been a few days of high pressure and it seemed fate was favouring the mission. Falcon and Antoine had found a spot in woodland to the north west of the railway yards, to observe proceedings.

Whatever night for the attack, the standing plan was for it to begin at 01:15. This gave full hours of darkness for the flight from England and back and it was hoped to catch the train shut up for the night. That was not what was happening in the train tonight, though. The blinds in the train were mostly drawn, but the blackout was far from complete and some windows were showing small slits of light. As the hour approached, a train door was flung open and figures emerged. They did not seem conscious of the blackout at all. In the light from the train, Falcon clearly identified Hartmann.

There were only minutes to go, if they were on time. Falcon noted that there was no air-raid warning yet. If the attackers were coming tonight, they were going to achieve complete surprise. The cars carrying the VIPs left, and the door of the train closed, shutting off the light which had glowed through the open door way.

Minutes passed. A door opened again, this time at the other end of the coach. The man who had come out stepped down from the train and looked round, as if searching the sky.

Falcon turned on the radio set to receive. Immediately he heard Rhys Evans *"Wyt ti'n barod?"*[8]

Falcon replied, *"Hebog. Ydyn Ydyn.Croeso!"*[9]

*

A group of four Mosquitoes including Evans and Woodward had flown at tree top height and high speed across France. It was a relatively clear night. Their speed and low level had apparently taken the defences unawares and they arrived over Strasbourg unmolested. The other three Mosquito aircraft stood off, circling at the edges of the city, observing and ready to follow up. Woodward gained a little height and circled himself, making out the landmarks of the river and the railway yards. The defenders would wake up any minute. In the clear air they could make out the bend of the river and identified that they were directly over the target spot. Woodward closed the throttles and turned away from the city, losing height. They would come in from the northwest at low level. Evans said, "Make sure you miss the chimneys this time!"

---

8 *"Are you ready?"*

9 *"Falcon Yes. Yes. Welcome!"*

*

Schultze scanned the sky. He was sure he heard a faint noise of aircraft. Then it fell silent. The hairs on the back of his neck prickled, but seeing and hearing nothing more, he started back up the steps. From the corner of his eye he noticed a light flicker somewhere across to his right. A light was moving across the railway yard. Where was it coming from? The light went out. An air raid siren started somewhere and at the same instant a dark shape burst across the sky with a roar that shocked him and shook the windows of the train. He froze on the steps leading back up to the train. The aircraft had passed over, but he knew what he must do. He bounded back into the coach and found Hartmann draining a brandy glass, having been shaken by the noise. "What was that?"

Schultze made no reply but ran down the coach opening the blinds.

"What do you think you are doing?" Hartmann blurted out. "Are you mad?"

*

On the run-in over the train at the height of the tree-tops and chimneys, Evans powered up the light, and it played over empty tracks and goods trucks standing idle. Some tiny weaving actions moved the light and they caught sight of the train, but a second too late to get shots in. Evans held his fire and killed the light.

Woodward stood the Mosquito on its wing tip for a tight 180 degree turn and they realigned the attack run. Searchlights were coming on, but pointing straight up. The defenders were confused where the attackers might be. Evans turned on the Leigh light again. Dead ahead, the train was now lit up like a Christmas tree from the open window blinds. Falcon was shouting instructions in a stream of enthusiastic Welsh. Evans did not need much help. The aiming spot from his light moved slowly along the train as he controlled the direction of the aircraft, until it lay over the illuminated coach.

Falcon saw Schultze return to the coach and the blinds being opened. He could clearly see Schultze and Hartmann remonstrating with him. He knew what to expect from the aiming light, but had left England before the installation was complete. His practices had been with the tracer streams. It was going to work. He kept up a commentary for Evans, while watching Schultze and Hartmann who were clearly visible inside the illuminated train. Even with the reflection in the train window, Falcon thought they must be able to see the source of the light pointing straight at them. It was a split second's thought.

The first shell from the Mosquito's big cannon passed clean through the train windows exploding on the other side, but in the blink of an eye it was followed by another and another round, until Falcon lost count. In the darkness the sheets of flame made spots in the eyes of the watchers Falcon and Antoine. The coach they had been studying had just disappeared in seconds. The attacking aircraft passed straight over the coach with a roar, and for the first and only time, they saw the belly of the swift twin-engined aircraft illuminated in the flames from the wreckage of the train.

All hell broke loose. Anti-aircraft fire from the ground began and searchlights criss-crossed the sky. More aeroplanes swept over the railway yard at low level and the area riven by explosions widened as the other Mosquitoes dropped bombs with a precision only achievable at low level. Around Falcon and Antoine, debris was falling back to earth from whatever was being thrown into the sky by the bombs that were cratering the site. They were much too close for comfort. Falcon spoke the code word "Volatile, Volatile" – and a final message in welsh. *Da iawn. R'oedd y seithi'n wych. Y targed ar dynion wedi eu difetha.*[10] Without waiting for a reply, he quickly shut down the radio as some large part of a railway wagon fell from the sky and thudded into the ground only a few yards away. Soon, it was going to be even more dangerous to be in this spot. They had prepared for this moment and had commandeered a motorcycle and side-car. The pair hauled the radio across to the bike and stuffed it into the side-car. They needed to put as much distance between them and the railway yard as they could. The streets were still largely deserted, but they did see two fire engines heading the other way. They were three or four miles away when more bombs started to rain down on the city. Mostly the explosions were back where they had come from, but some were close by. They turned into a spot close by the river. The short but useful life of the radio had come to an end. It had to be destroyed as soon as possible. They dumped it by the water's edge, pushed it half into the mud and set the fuse for the destruct charges housed in the radio that would ignite a high temperature incendiary within the casing. The timer was less than a minute and they stood back and watched it blossom into flame, so bright that it could not be looked at in the dark, even against the glow in the distance originating from the railway yard where they had been minutes before. Another stick of bombs shook the ground – they were still too close for the inaccuracy of the high-level attack from the heavy bombers thousands of feet above them. They resumed their retreat with all haste.

*

In the cockpit of the mosquito Evans was quickly retracting the light with the tube on its mounting when he heard the message

10 *"Well done. Good shooting. Target and personnel destroyed."*

from Falcon "Volatile", followed by his congratulations in Welsh. The message confirmed Woodward's opinion of their success. Sometimes in precision attacks in daylight, you did actually see what you were shooting at, but it was unusual at night. They were wondering why the blackout had been so poor and the men inside so easy to spot, but at that second, the cockpit was briefly lit up by a ground search light. There was splintering above the sound of engines and shock to the airframe that they felt through the seats. Their speed and low altitude quickly took them out of the beam.

Woodward involuntarily stated the obvious. "We've been hit!"

Rhys responded more in hope than expectation. "Still flying though!"

Woodward said, "Send the bloody message that we've done it – while we can."

Evans relayed the success code word back to base and to the other aircraft – it was unlikely that it would be picked up directly.

Woodward was feeling the controls, testing the response of the aircraft and looking at the dim glow of the instruments in the darkness. He was flying level and low in a south easterly direction and away from the immediate danger area.

"The old kite is responding ok still" said Woodward as he tried weaving the aircraft. "Have a look round."

Evans looked out to see a stream of fluid in their wake, reflected in the moonlight and the receding flames of the railway yard. He pointed it out to Woodward.

"I think they've hit the fuel tanks."

They both stared at the fuel gauge – it was lower than when last checked and was creeping downwards almost perceptibly as they watched.

Evans asked flatly, "We're not going to get home, are we?"

"I should say not. Sod it."

*

Ron waited in the control room. The other Mosquitoes were the first back, followed by the heavy bombers – they put down at Whittingsmoor as dawn approached. Evans and Woodward were not among the returning aircraft. Ron asked the flight controller, "Where is Woodward? Has he put down somewhere else?" Often crews ended up at the wrong station after a raid, due to damage, or weather, or navigation problems. The flight controller shook his head. With a heavy heart, Ron made his way over to the briefing room.

The crews assembled for the debrief looking shattered as they always did. Sometimes they flew longer distances, to Berlin for instance, but flying on a clear night in moonlight was not the most popular mission. Five aircraft had failed to return, four heavies and Woodward and Evans.

The other crews had heard the transmissions to and from Evans, although none had understood anything except the code word "Volatile", which they had been asked to listen out for. No one had heard the alternative "Underground" that would have signified failure.

Nicholson listened to the debrief silently in the corner of the room, while the intelligence officers tried to extract as much information as possible from the tired crews, before they went off for breakfast.

Ron struggled with his emotions, which were mostly guilt. Guilt at not feeling more sorry about the other missing crews, some of whom he vaguely knew, but mostly guilt at getting the chaps into this, especially Rhys Evans – a young man who he had taken under his wing.

As the aircrew left, Nicholson got up and clapped Ron on the back, but sensing Ron's emotions, then put his arm around his shoulders. "Looks like a big success. We are certain that the target has been destroyed. That's the end of Prof Hartmann. It's what your boys wanted to do – and maybe we'll hear from them yet. You heard the other crews – we know they kept flying for a while, before they lost contact."

It seemed a faint hope and feeble encouragement for the loss that Ron felt at that moment.

*

The Oberleutnant made a report to his Abwehr superiors. "There was a British bomber raid on Strassburg last night. Their target seems to have been the railway junctions in Strassburg. There has been quite a bit of damage. It will disrupt the railway network for some time."

The Rittmeister looked up from his desk. "This is very inconvenient, but not surprising. The British have been targeting our railway yards. I think this affects our transport into France doesn't it?"

"Yes. There is more news Sir."

"Not more bad news I hope."

"Prof Hartmann's mobile research facility was in Strassburg last night. It seems it was pretty much caught up in the raid. We can't even find the wreckage."

"Hartmann – eh? Maybe the bad news is not that bad." Hartmann was not universally popular with some sections of the Abwehr. The senior officer stubbed out a cigarette and exhaled with an air of resignation. "It puts an end to Hartmann's theories about coding, code breaking and all that. It was a diversion from the main business of the war. Ironic that his ideas of avoiding raids by not having a fixed base has had the opposite effect. Still, we had indulged him for long enough. Perhaps we'll worry less about academic exercises and more about getting enough resources for the Wehrmacht."

*

Nicholson was summoned for a meeting on the operation. He found Dr James and Smith in attendance. James kicked off straight way. "Your operation has had some interesting outcomes."

Smith commented. "By and large a good success I would say."

Nicholson said nothing, guessing this was a wrap-up at the end of the project.

James carried on. "Yes. It's pretty obvious from our Enigma interceptions that the Germans have bought the whole thing lock stock and barrel. It's completely accepted that the raid that eliminated their coding investigation team was incidental to the raid on the Strasbourg railway yards. From the intercepts, it also seems that certain members of the German military won't mourn his passing.

Smith added, "The overwhelming view that prevails is that Enigma is completely secure, so I think that Station X can continue to operate in its present form for some time. Of course that doesn't mean their work is easy and we still need to keep capturing codes and code books. But it would have been fatal if Hartmann had carried on and got his way." He paused. "Although it all worked, the whole thing has been too risky. You've only knocked two people off the list – we think it is not the way to do it. The special section – air operations of SOE(A) is to be disbanded."

Nicholson was not surprised, but it was a blow of sorts as he had pulled the team and the operation together. "Phew. It was a lot of work to chuck away."

James was positive. "Not all lost. There were a number of innovations that were proven. We are thinking about using the cannon against submarines. This was the original idea anyway and you have just shown the possibilities. The light is already doing well in the same situation, but needs more development for use over land – we're thinking of an infra-red beam so it won't be seen."

Nicholson was professional and expressed his professional concern. "But we did lose our Oboe-fitted aircraft and the cannon and the light. All things we really prefer the Germans didn't know about."

Smith had some news on that. "Ah." He took out an envelope and passed it over the desk. "Have a look at this message from Switzerland. It's from our embassy in Berne."

*

The special assignment over, Ron was back at his desk in the orderly room, but with more rank than when he started. Only reverse justice maybe – he had set up himself one of the best offices in the base, even when he was a sergeant. Joan sat on the other side of the desk and Sally from the orderly room team brought in two mugs of tea.

One of the ubiquitous manila files was on the desk marked 'Most Secret'. Ron nodded towards it. "It seems you were right about

Wolfgang. The report says he deliberately placed himself in the line of fire by lighting up the train to be targeted. Our agents saw him."

Joan sipped her tea. "So he made his own decision – your conscience can be clear."

"I suppose so. That doesn't make it any easier with this letter I'm trying to write to Evan's family in Wales."

"And I suppose the reason it's difficult is not because it's in Welsh?"

"No, that's not the reason, as you might guess."

Sally knocked on the door. "Message from Group Captain Ryland. He said to ring him when you could. Shall I get him for you now?

Ron never delayed a call to the boss. "Yes please, Sally."

The phone rang a couple of minutes later. When Ron picked it up and before he had a chance to speak, he heard Ryland say, "Has your girl given you an envelope?"

Ron said, "Sorry Sir, envelope Sir?"

Sally knocked and came back in, handing an envelope to Ron. Ah, yes Sir, she's giving it to me now." Sally went back out and closed the door.

Joan thought Ron looked puzzled. She heard Ron say "Thank you, Sir." As he put down the phone Ron said, "Ryland said I might like this."

He slit open the envelope and started reading silently. Very silently.

Joan asked, "Am I allowed to know?"

In response, Ron stood up, opened his office door and stood in the doorway, so that Sally, the other WAAFs and the two Airmen working in the outer office could hear him speak. "Listen everyone."

Ron read from the official RAF signal. '*While on operations over Germany, the Mosquito aircraft of Sergeant Woodward and Airman Evans was hit by enemy fire and severely damaged. Showing great skill and determination, Sergeant Woodward flew the aircraft into neutral Switzerland and made a controlled ditching.*'

Ron paused, finding it difficult to speak for a moment, but took the time to unfold a second sheet. You could have heard a pin drop in the office.

"This is a memo from the British Embassy in Berne. He read '*We are in receipt of a complaint about a violation of Swiss airspace. The Swiss authorities report that a belligerent British aeroplane flew into Switzerland and crashed into Lake Klingnau in Canton Aargau, where it immediately sank. The crew, namely British Royal Air Force persons Woodward 1478094 and Evans 2064771 parachuted to the ground before the crash and being uninjured were taken into custody by the Cantonal authorities.*"

Ron was interrupted by a huge cheer from the men and women in the office. He resumed with some emotion, "*In accordance with international law, and as members of belligerent forces in neutral territory, they will be interned in Switzerland for the duration of hostilities*.

Over the applause Ron added. "The note also tells us that Airman Ryhs Evans has expressed a wish to work in agriculture during his internment and is currently tending livestock on Swiss uplands."

"It seems there's been a welcome in the hills – the hills of Switzerland!"

THE END

Lightning Source UK Ltd.
Milton Keynes UK
UKHW03f1017230318
319940UK00006B/105/P

9 781787 196889